# THE★SHOW

# THE★SHOW

## I'm With Cupid

by Jordan Cooke

Grosset & Dunlap

GROSSET & DUNLAP
Published by the Penguin Group
Penguin Group (USA) Inc., 375 Hudson Street, New York, New York 10014, USA
Penguin Group (Canada), 90 Eglinton Avenue East, Suite 700, Toronto, Ontario
M4P 2Y3, Canada (a division of Pearson Penguin Canada Inc.)
Penguin Books Ltd., 80 Strand, London WC2R 0RL, England
Penguin Group Ireland, 25 St. Stephen's Green, Dublin 2, Ireland
(a division of Penguin Books Ltd.)
Penguin Group (Australia), 250 Camberwell Road, Camberwell, Victoria 3124, Australia
(a division of Pearson Australia Group Pty. Ltd.)
Penguin Books India Pvt. Ltd., 11 Community Centre, Panchsheel Park,
New Delhi—110 017, India
Penguin Group (NZ), 67 Apollo Drive, Rosedale, North Shore 0632, New Zealand
(a division of Pearson New Zealand Ltd.)
Penguin Books (South Africa) (Pty.) Ltd., 24 Sturdee Avenue,
Rosebank, Johannesburg 2196, South Africa

Penguin Books Ltd., Registered Offices: 80 Strand, London WC2R 0RL, England

Cover designed by Ching N. Chan.
Front cover image © Spring Break/Fancy Photography/Veer Inc.
Back cover image © Agnieszka Pastuszak-Maksim/iStockphoto/iStock International Inc.

Library of Congress Cataloging-in-Publication Data is available.

ISBN 978-0-448-44688-2          10 9 8 7 6 5 4 3 2 1

# The 'Bu \ thə boo\

1: popular nickname for California's
legendary Malibu Beach, as in Malibu.
2: the hottest teen beach drama ever to hit
TV land (see inside for actual script pages).
3: a complete and utter freak show.

# Prologue

**High Above It All—Early September, 1:12 A.M.**

## The Bu-Hoo

*'Bu* ba-hay-bies!

It's your old pal, MBK. Haven't heard from me in a while, have ya? What can I say? After those crazazy *'Bu* tykes finished filming their "very special" live second episode, I figured I needed a couple weeks off.

**CAN YA BLAME ME????**

So did I go to the desert and shoot coyotes?
Nah.

Did I Jeep it up to Big Bear and commune with
big bears? Nu-uh.

What did I do, you ask? Poor MBK was so
stressed out after the last month in *'Bu*-land, I got
me a cheapo shrink and went into therapy!
PAGING DR. PHIL!

I mean all that *'Bu* crying? All those *'Bu*
confessions? MBK was wiped out!

Tanya Ventura is not a virgin after all—and then
gets *revirginized* for the sake of her career????

Anushka "Champagne Breath" Peters trying to
make it as a *college girl*??? HA!

Corliss "Clueless" Meyers saying NO to a
psychology major at Columbia University and
YES to a demonology major in Hollyweird????

Trent Owen Michaels's HYSTERICAL Jenny Craig diet (can you say "starch intake," surfer boy??).

Rocco DiTullio's RIOTOUS 'roid abuse (ruin camera equipment much???).

Jonathan "Master" Bader's WAY GEEKY day-trading habit (can't you get a REAL addiction, dude????).

Of course, now they all CLAIM things are brazilliant in *'Bu*-land and everyone's back to work all huggy and kissy.

## WHICH I HATE.

It makes my job soooooooo hard. Give me the dramz! Give me JB spending all his mom's money online! Give me Rocco in a 'roid rage! Give me Anushka passing fake ID! Give me Trent scarfing carbs! Give me Tanya uncrossing her legs!

## IS ALL THAT TOO MUCH TO ASK??????

But I'm here to tell ya: All this good behavior can't

last forever. One of those naughty 'Bu kids will certainly screw up ROYALLY before long. MARK MY WORDS. And when they do, you know I'll be there!

Yours 'Buly,
MBK

# One

The sun was just coming out from behind a bank of slate gray clouds. The beach was windswept, photo-ready, postcard-approved. Pieces of driftwood dotted the shoreline, art directed to perfection. *The 'Bu* machine had been in full force all morning to create the perfect SoCal tableau, and the first shot of the day was up. Dozens of technicians held their breath. The cast did, too. Tanya, sporting an edibly delicious Alexander McQueen micro-bikini, was frozen mid-hair twirl. Trent, packed into Tom Ford board shorts, lanky and blond, slouched at her side. Rocco, his inky black hair wet and clinging to his massive neck, stood ready, looking like Atlas. JB, swimming in Billabongs two sizes too big, waited on tiptoes, adorable and totally wired-for-geek at the same time. And at the center of them all: one very unhappy starlet named Anushka.

"Anushka," said Max, standing under a Bottega Veneta umbrella held up by one of his identically dressed assistants, "are you ready now? We've finally got the sun and we'd like to shoot."

Anushka, who was wearing a pink Bianca Nero bikini the size of three postage stamps, let out a long, disdainful breath. "Max, with all due respect, I told you I wouldn't be ready until my eyebrows were fixed. One is up WAY higher than the other. So this side looks all surprised"—she pointed to one eye—"and this side looks all sleepy-time"—she pointed to the other. She turned to Corliss. "Back me up here, Cor. The Emmys are coming up in a couple weeks and I'm NOT walking the red carpet looking like this, that's for sure."

Corliss—who was looking mighty cute in a pleated peach Temperley London sundress and Dolce Vita Mary Jane shoes—tried to smile. This had been Anushka's second diva display of the day. One hour before, she'd requested an emergency pedicure after stubbing her toe on a conch shell. And her toes weren't even in the shot! Time was already slowing to a crawl on the set—and Corliss knew this was *exactly* Max's biggest fear about hiring Anushka back on *The 'Bu*. But Max didn't seem fazed. In fact, he was smiling enigmatically.

"Anushka," he said, "I can have Tatiana in hair and makeup here in two minutes with a pair of twenty-four-karat gold tweezers. She can make your eyebrows even. She can make them look like lightning bolts. She can put them on the back of your head if you like." His odd, infinitely patient smile continued. "Just say the word."

Anushka glared through her uneven eyebrows. "I don't want *Tatiana*, Max," said Anushka. "She's the one who made me look like some pinkeye victim in the first place. I want Urich!"

Corliss gritted her teeth. Urich, the legendary—and way expensive—stylist Anushka had made Max hire, had gone missing somewhere between Laguna Beach and the Desert Hills outlet stores. Anushka would not be pleased to hear that wholesale shopping prices had come between her and evenly arched eyebrows.

"Anushka," said Corliss, stepping forward to supply whatever white lie popped out of her mouth. "Urich had a, uh, salon emergency. Go figure, right?" Corliss slapped her palm against her forehead and laughed, hoping that Anushka would, too.

"Salon emergency?" barked Anushka. "What's that— when Ashley Tisdale cuts her bangs too short? Cor, what do you take me for? I spent half the pilot episode looking like a fashion-challenged bag lady. I am NOT going to make my comeback to *The 'Bu* with cockeyed eyebrows!"

Corliss leaned in to Max and whispered, "Anushka's a little on edge today because she found out her reality show got put on hold by Fox. One of the producers had second thoughts about dropping her in the Brazilian rain forest to live among the indigenous reptile population."

"Guess he was worried for the reptiles," Max whispered back. Corliss stifled a giggle.

"Excuse me with the whispering?" said Anushka, putting one hand on one exquisitely toned hip.

"Anushka," said Max in a level tone. "Let's take ten. If

we can't find Urich by then, I have some books on creative visualization in my trailer that might be of some assistance." With that, he turned and signaled for Corliss and his identically dressed assistants to follow.

As the entourage moved toward Max's trailer, Corliss looked back. Anushka did not look happy; she *hated* it whenever people didn't take her diva bait. "I gotta say, Max, you handled that really well," said Corliss, catching up to him. "You didn't get all frazzled and go into your girly voice. You let Anushka know who's boss."

"Thank you, Corliss. I've realized if I want a productive set, I'm going to have to keep Anushka on a very tight leash. I'm also going to have to take testosterone enhancers to keep my voice low."

"I think you're on to something, Max. Two things, in fact."

"Perhaps," Max said, approaching his trailer. "But believe it or not, Corliss, I have more pressing concerns at the moment." His face became serious. Way more serious than it usually was. He signaled for his assistants to move off. They flew away in unison.

"Is it the fact that all your assistants always dress exactly like you? 'Cause it kinda creeps me out. How do they even know what you're going to wear every day?"

"They generally call or text me early in the morning and I tell them. I can't help it if they want to be like me, Corliss. Imitation is, after all, the sincerest form of flattery. But no, my pressing concern has nothing to do with them."

"Then what is it, Max?" Corliss and Max were now standing just outside his trailer.

"It's almost so terrible I can't even talk about it." With that, Max flung open the door to his trailer. There, sitting inside the trailer on the floor, was Legend.

"Hey, Corlith!" He was just as Corliss remembered him, with a nose bludgeoned from some serious nose-picking and wearing one of his signature T-shirts. This one said I AM THE AFTERPARTY.

Corliss gulped. She hadn't laid eyes on the bite-sized terror in weeks. And those had been some good weeks. "Hey, Legend," she said carefully. "What—what are you doing there?"

"Oh, nothing. Juth making a drawing on my Etch A Thketch." He held up his Etch A Sketch. Max's face went white. Corliss gasped. She hadn't seen anything so graphic since she'd walked into a Venice Beach men's room by mistake.

"Legend," gasped Max, "where did you learn to draw THAT?"

"From the pictureth in your creative vithualithathion book . . ." he said, looking the picture of perverted innocence.

Max swiped Legend's Etch A Sketch and shook it quickly to make the image disappear. Then he shut the door and took Corliss away from the trailer.

"Hey!" called Legend from inside. "You erathed my penith picture!"

"Sorry you had to see that, Corliss. There's a chapter in my creative visualization book about, um, making love, and I think, well . . ."

"Relax, Max, it's not the first time I've seen a penis." The minute she heard herself say this she paused. "Except for when I wandered into a Venice Beach bathroom by mistake and—"

Max held up his talk-to-the-hand. "Corliss, way TMI. But now you see my terrible problem. It's Legend. My parents have left town again."

"Vegas for the week?"

"South Africa for the month!" Max's voice leaped to his girly register. "They're in Botswana helping Oprah open a school for the 'differently abled.' Legend's nanny quit on them the day they were leaving. I offered to take care of him while they're gone, but he's driving me crazy. This morning he put soy milk in my Kiehl's Olive Fruit Oil Nourishing Shampoo. That's why my hair is flat and inconsistent. Don't say you haven't noticed."

*Actually*, thought Corliss, *Max's hair did look a little mashed to one side.* "First of all, your hair looks great, Max," she said, knowing she always had to lie where his hair was concerned. "And second, there must be a ton of nanny agencies in L.A. you could call."

"Of course there are, Corliss, but then you have to *interview* nannies. I don't have time now that we're in production on the third '*Bu* episode. You understand the—how do I put this—*specialness* of my stepbrother Legend. Would you please do the legwork here? Call a few agencies? Check out a few nannies? Or mannies? It doesn't matter to me. Just someone appropriate for a five-year-old with behavioral issues, a chronic speech impediment, and a serious nose-picking problem."

"But Max," said Corliss, trying to remain calm in the face of his request—a request that had *nothing* to do with her official duties as his first assistant on *The 'Bu*. "How can I find Legend a nanny when I have to function as a liaison between you and the cast, you and the writers, and you and your identically dressed assistants? I mean, didn't I prove myself professionally by helping with the live 'Bu episode? Isn't that why you hired me in a semiofficial capacity? I put off going to school, even! Do you really think my job description should include nanny-getting?" Corliss stood tall. She wasn't going to back down. But then she realized Mary Janes might not have been the best footwear choice on a day she needed to take a stand.

"I appreciate your sacrifices, Corliss," said Max finally. "And thank you for saying my hair looks good just a moment ago, but if Legend is underfoot, I won't be able to do my work. Which means I'll have meltdowns. Which means I'll take it out on the cast and writers. Which means you'll have more work than you already do."

Corliss was dumbstruck. Max was right. "The last thing I need is more work," she said, shuddering as she pictured seventeen-hour workdays. "I've already diagnosed myself with workaholic tendencies—which has me looking at a good half-year of therapy once I can afford it!"

"Does that mean you'll help find a nanny for Legend?"

Corliss sighed. There was no way out. Either she had to find Legend a nanny or deal with an emotionally maxed-out Max. "I guess I have to help here, Max. But I could really use some man power. Can you spare a few of your assistants? With all the responsibilities I already have, I won't have time to do all the nanny research myself."

"Avail yourself of whichever assistants you need," said Max, taking Corliss by the arms with a look of profound gratitude. "I can't tell them apart, anyway, so I won't know who's missing. And thank you, Corliss. To show my gratitude, I'm going to ask the head office if they can swing a couple tickets for you for the Emmys. The whole cast is going—why shouldn't my first assistant go as well?"

Corliss gulped. The Emmys! And *two* tickets. "Max, are you serious? What will I wear? Who will I bring?!"

Before Max could respond, his trailer door slammed open and Legend stood there, smiling demonically, showing off his most recent Etch A Sketch masterpiece. "Hey, look what I drew!" Max's eyes bulged. Corliss had to look away.

This time Legend had Etch A Sketched a *vagina* masterpiece.

"Corliss!" screamed Max in a voice so high no testosterone in the world could lower it. "Please grab that creative visualization book from him right now!"

## The Production Trailer—Twenty Minutes Later

The place was crammed with Max's assistants, all of whom were scowling at Corliss. They all hated her because she was Max's favorite. And because she didn't feel the need to dress, act, or cut her hair like Max just to appeal to his ego. She had her brains and can-do attitude. They only had a talent for butt-kissing.

Corliss immediately regretted asking for their assistance.

"Okay, here's the deal," she said, trying her best to summon an air of authority. "Everyone search the following websites: Nannys4hire.com, SoCalKidKeepers.net, and, well, for good measure"—she consulted the list she'd made—"Cabananannies.org. When you find a suitable candidate to take care of Legend, raise your hand and I'll come over."

They all made tight little smiles at Corliss—the kind that said, "None of us like you"—and then moved to the banks of computers that lined the trailer. Corliss ignored their cranky little clone faces and sat down at the big desk, the one Max usually used whenever he was in the production office. Which was never.

*Okay*, she thought, signing on to the computer in front of her, *I need to find a nanny who's patient, strong-willed, and gross-out resistant. Whoever takes care of Legend is going to have to be all of the above.*

The tap-tap-tapping of typing filled the trailer as Max's assistants competed with one another to see who could come up with a nanny candidate first. Corliss smiled to herself. It came pretty easily to her to give Max's assistants directions. She wondered if down the line she might have *her own* staff of clones . . . She imagined all Max's assistants wearing the sundress she'd put on that morning. They looked kind of cute in them. Even the boys. But an unwelcome sight quickly quashed her daydream . . .

"Hey, Corliss!" said Petey Newsome, as raccoon-eyed and dressed head-to-toe in black as ever. He was standing just inside the trailer.

Corliss gasped. She couldn't imagine why in the world Petey would be there. She'd thought for sure she'd seen the last of him when Max found out he was underage and his contract as a 'Bu writer had been declared null and void. "Petey, what are you doing here?"

"What do you mean?" he said, looking as if nothing had ever happened. "I'm working, of course."

"WHAT?" Corliss's mind did loop-di-loops. Had Petey been *hired back*? And if he had been, did that mean he'd be chasing her around the beach again, pining for her unrequited love? It was too much to contemplate. "But—but—last I heard you were a fry chef at El Coyote!"

Petey looked at the floor. "Well, yeah, but I dropped my inhaler in the fryer one night. I got fired when a piece of it turned up in George Clooney's gordita."

Corliss's stomach lurched. The thought of George Clooney chowing down on Petey's deep-fried inhaler was way too much. Max's assistants made "Eww-that's-gross" faces and turned back to the computers. "But Petey," said Corliss, her mind racing to make sense of this development, "you're not eighteen. You *can't* be working here."

He smiled his crooked, weird smile at Corliss. "Well, an amazing thing happened, Corliss," Petey droned. "I was so demoralized after the gordita incident that I marched myself over to Max Marx's office and begged for my job back. I told him I'd work for free until I was eighteen—which is only a month away. He said sure. I'm now once again on the writing staff of *The 'Bu*. Isn't that great?"

"Yeah," said Corliss, trying to hide how not great she thought it was.

"And it's especially great to see *you*, Corliss. You look pretty in that sundress."

Max's assistants giggled. Corliss was mortified. She certainly didn't want any rumors flying around about them. "Er, thanks, Petey, but we're a little busy in here," she said, gesturing at Max's assistants, who were now once again furiously tapping away at various nanny sites.

"Of course," said Petey sheepishly. "Don't let me be a bother." He started inching out the door, but then stopped and turned back. "Um, maybe we could hang out tonight after work? Head down to the Malibu Shopping Center and get an oatmeal cookie at Marmalade Café? Or some chicken strips at Googies?"

Corliss's stomach lurched again. The thought of eating *anything* in the near vicinity of the personal-hygiene-challenged Petey made her woozy. Max's assistants started to giggle again, but Corliss shot them a look. "Um, Petey, could we talk when there aren't a whole bunch of people around listening?"

"Oh," said Petey. "I get it—a little alone time for Corliss and Petey?"

"NO! I mean—look—I'll come find you on my next break, okay?"

"Okay," said Petey, smiling his crooked, strange smile. "See you soon."

As Petey stepped out of the trailer, Corliss immediately called Max. He picked up on the second ring. "Corliss, have you already found a nanny?"

"No, Max, I'm calling because I want to know why you hired Petey back! I mean, I know I did that lousy rewrite for you, but sheesh! This town is full of writers you could have hired! He's so weird with his insomnia eyes, and he makes me feel all oogy—"

"Corliss—"

"—and he's always up in my grill! Which means he always wants to go out with me, and I'm, like, blech, no way!" All of Max's assistants were once again giggling. "I'm sorry, Max," she said. "But I can't find Legend a nanny and avoid the unwelcome advances of Petey McWeirdo at the same time! There's only so much Corliss to go around!"

"Corliss, you're having a fit. You must calm down. Try some deep breathing, or look at that creative visualization book I had you take away from Legend."

"I did, Max, but all it did was make me think of how babies are made! I couldn't help but imagine what a baby fathered by Petey Newsome would look like, which only made me feel worse!"

"Not *that* chapter, Corliss. The chapter that tells you how to imagine yourself in a safe space. I'm imagining myself in an Internet-equipped igloo as we speak."

"That's completely weird, Max."

"Perhaps, but I'm as cheerful as a plugged-in Eskimo. Now as for Petey, the truth is he's a good writer. And we're getting him for free. Cheap labor makes the network happy. If Petey makes you that uncomfortable, I'll just implement a dating embargo. Absolutely no fraternizing between any 'Bu employees. Cast, crew—you name it."

"You'd do that?! Boy, that would really take the burn off, Max."

"It's as good as done," replied Max.

"But wait—what about Trent and Tanya?"

"Well, it's obviously too late for them. But that doesn't mean I'm not still carefully monitoring their relationship. I've got our beloved boss, one Mr. Michael Rothstein, breathing down my neck about those two ever since the live episode. Trent and Tanya could do a lot of damage if they have a falling-out. Which is yet another reason there should be no dating among the staff. So my mind is made up: There is no dating allowed between *anyone* working on *The 'Bu* from this point forward."

"Thank you SO much, Max."

"Say no more about it. Just get back to work finding a nanny—and pronto."

"Absolutely, Captain," said Corliss, saluting the phone.

"Uh-oh . . ."

"What is it, Max?" Corliss could hear a strange noise in the background. "Is that screaming . . . ?"

"I'm afraid it is, Corliss. Legend is with me on set and he just figured out how to unhook Tanya's bikini top. She's having a fit—and now Anushka's storming off in a huff . . . We need to creatively visualize a nanny and pronto!"

Max disconnected. Corliss took a big breath and went back to the nanny search. With Petey out of her hair, and Max's assistants no longer giggling, she was feeling her can-do attitude coming back, full force.

## Hair and Makeup Trailer—Fifteen Minutes Later

"Anushka, *please*," said Max in his most beseeching tone. "We've fixed your eyebrows. Now what's the problem?"

Anushka spun around in the makeup chair and looked him dead in the eye. Her eyebrows had indeed been fixed. They both now arched gorgeously over her lionlike lunar blue eyes. But her famous hair—those buckwheat tresses that flounced around her perfect shoulders, the hair that captured hearts from Burbank to Basra—was nowhere to be found. In fact, she was as bald as baboon's behind. "You are seriously going to look at my head, Max, and ask me *what's the problem*?"

Max knew he had to keep his voice low and confident if he was to convey authority. He made a note in his iPhone to call his doctor about a testosterone enhancer. When he looked up from his note-jotting, he realized Anushka was about to blow sky-high. The hair and makeup people began to slowly back up, like customers in a bank robbery trying to judge the exact moment they might begin running for their lives. Max decided the best thing to do was pretend Anushka's bald head wasn't such a big deal. "What, Anushka? I think you look cute."

"You think I look . . . *cute*? I look like Britney Spears on a bender! I come to hair and makeup to get my eyebrows evened out and then—as a joke, I assume—they start putting a bald cap on me and then you come in and tell me it's not a joke and that I LOOK CUTE!!"

The hair and makeup people fled the trailer. Max was left alone with his ranting starlet. "Now, Anushka, please hear me out."

She crossed her arms over her magnificent chest and waited. As she did, her eyes seemed to shoot rays of rage into Max's very soul. Not telling Anushka about the bald cap in advance was a serious misstep. Max thought for certain he'd asked Corliss to break it to her so she wouldn't be surprised. He quickly texted Corliss: REPORT TO HAIR AND MAKEUP *ASAP*.

"Anushka, the writers went to great lengths to come up with a reason why your character, Alecia, could come back to the show after supposedly perishing in the fire. They decided a young woman was killed in the fire and burned beyond recognition. Her body was thought to be your character, Alecia. But Alecia, it turns out, was hiding in the canyon, subsisting off forest brush and rainwater."

"Ha!" Anushka barked contemptuously. "As if I could ever live without Pinkberry!"

"Please, Anushka, don't interrupt. Alecia couldn't possibly have emerged from such a major fire unscathed, so the writers decided the fire burned all her hair off."

"Uh, a bit drastic?" she said sarcastically.

"Not if you consider that they first suggested you come back as an amputee."

"What?!"

"Calm down, Anushka. I told them America doesn't want to see an amputee in a bikini. They might, however, want to see one beautiful girl, surviving against all odds—bald, but unbroken."

Anushka pretended to weep as she played a tiny, invisible violin. "I get it. I read the script, Max. Survivor, loved by all—yada

yada. But there's one problem, and it's a BIG one. I consented to come back to *The 'Bu* on one condition. And that condition is that no matter what the scene—no matter what I was doing in it—no matter how late at night or early in the morning it was shot, I was going to be HOT. H-O-T, Max."

"But," he said, trying to resummon his patience, "how could you ever *not* look hot, Anushka? You're America's Hot Sweetheart. At least that's what *Star* magazine called you last week."

Anushka rose from her makeup chair and looked directly into Max's eyes. *"BALD IS NOT HOT!"*

Corliss arrived breathless, climbing up into the trailer. "What is it, Max? I came as fast as I—" And then she saw Anushka. "Uh-oh." She looked at Max. Her face registered her horror at what she'd forgotten to do. "With all the nanny business this morning I guess I forget to talk to Anushka about the, um"— Corliss gulped—"hair thing."

Max nodded solemnly. "I see, Corliss." He sighed. "Well, I guess I *have* been throwing a lot at you. Something was bound to get lost in the shuffle. It's just a shame it's the, um, 'hair thing'—as you so eloquently put it."

"YOU knew about this, Cor?" stammered Anushka, who was now shooting rage rays in Corliss's direction. "YOU were part of this ugly conspiracy?!"

"Don't blame Corliss, Anushka," said Max. "She's in the midst of an extremely high-level task for me. In any event, you need to know how important Alecia's baldness is to the plot. Especially when you hear how there's going to be a big scene for her when all her friends gather to tell her how they've been lost without her."

Anushka leaped from the makeup chair and banged toward the trailer door. "Another nice try, Max. A big hospital scene with tears—*blah, blah, blah*—no one can live without me—*whatevs.* But none of that," she said, jutting her cleavage forward so Max could get the point, "makes me look *HOT*. I don't care if I'm hooked up to twelve IVs, getting blood transfusions through my ears, and hanging on to life by a *thread*—if I'm not covered in hotness and camera-ready, I walk! *Comprendo?*"

"Anushka," said Corliss, "don't go! I'm sorry!"

But Anushka was already out the door.


## The Beach—Continuous

Anushka marched toward her trailer, kicking up a cloud of sand as she went. Corliss trudged behind her. Max followed. "Anushka," said Corliss, "don't go getting your thong in a twist. Think of all the beautiful actresses who've won awards just by looking butt-ugly, right?"

Anushka stopped running. Max and Corliss stopped running. "Name 'em," said Anushka, steam practically shooting out of her ears.

Corliss cleared her throat and began. "Well, Jennifer Hudson in *Dreamgirls* had to play all frumpy. And Angelina Jolie had to wear that bag-lady wig in that movie nobody saw. *And*, at the very top of the list, America Ferrera has to play ugly in *Ugly Betty*!" Max examined Anushka's face closely. Corliss's argument seemed to be having an effect. "America Ferrera is so pretty in real life," Corliss continued, "but then on TV she looks like *Extreme Makeunder*. All of those women have shelves full of awards. In fact, being made to look ugly is practically the first step to getting an award in this town, if you think about it."

Max could tell Anushka was doing exactly that. "Let me do the math here . . ." she said. After a moment of raising and lowering her now-even eyebrows, she began to skip back to the hair and makeup trailer, a bald sandstorm in motion. Max and Corliss followed as best they could, spitting sand as they went.

## Hair and Makeup Trailer—Continuous

Anushka landed in front of the largest mirror in the trailer, cocking her chrome dome this way and that in contemplation. Max sighed at the sight. Even completely bald, Anushka could still stop traffic. In fact, her eyes looked otherworldly beautiful under her naked noggin—and her lips looked luscious and more kissable than ever. Max saw Corliss seeing this, too. But most importantly, he saw Anushka seeing it.

He watched as she picked up a bottle of Bed Head Spoil Me Defrizzer and cradled it like an Emmy Award, silently mouthing "thank you"s to all the little people, blowing kisses, nodding humbly. One single tear even fell and bounced off her bikini top.

Finally, Anushka slammed down the defrizzer and nodded. "Okay, Max. If being fugly is what it's going to take to get me any respect in this town—and an Emmy nomination—then I'm in."

Max and Corliss applauded simultaneously.

"Hold your applause!" She looked like she meant business. Max and Corliss did as they were told. "There are three conditions. Numero uno: I do this bald thing for *one* episode and *one episode only*. And numero two-o: I'm in a different Zac Posen micro-bikini for every scene I'm in. And numero three-o: Tanya is totally covered up for every scene *she's* in with me. Preferably in something unflattering and shapeless. Like a burka. Or a parka. Or a burka/parka. It could be a whole new look for her. Ha!"

Corliss looked at Max and shrugged. Max wondered how he could consent to such conditions. "But Anushka, we were supposed to start shooting this morning and you're in six scenes. I'm not sure the costume designer can handle *six* Zac Posens for you and something unflattering for Tanya on such short notice."

"Not my problem, Max," said Anushka, elbowing Corliss and winking as Max squirmed.

"Let me call the costume designer," he said, looking at Corliss, who nodded encouragingly. He placed the call to the designer. "Kennedy? This is Max Marx. We need six different Zac Posen micro-bikinis for Anushka, and something unflattering for Tanya. Will that be a problem?" He covered the phone. "She's checking." He listened again. "I see. Well, let me get back to you." He disconnected the call. "She says she can dress Tanya down for today's scenes but that she only has *two* Zac Posen micro-bikinis on the racks."

"No deal," said Anushka emphatically.

"I figured as much," said Max. "Then you leave me no choice, Anushka. Kennedy needs until tomorrow. We'll have to bump filming until the morning. But if I agree to this, that means I want to see you at 6 A.M. in this very chair looking bald as a baby's behind. Do we have a deal?"

"It's a deal, Max," said Anushka, peeling off her bald cap and shaking out her long locks. "If anyone needs me before then, I'll be at Barney Greengrass ordering the sturgeon scramble."

As she sashayed out the door, her perfect little bikini butt waving in the breeze, Corliss sighed. "Anushka catastrophe averted, Max!"

"For the moment," he said with a sinking feeling.

# Two

## The Hollywood Hills—10:13 P.M., That Night

Tanya thought her heart might burst into a million pink stars. She and Trent were parked in his new Toyota FJ Cruiser looking out over the glittering Los Angeles valley. They'd been making out for so long her lips were twice their normal puffy size. As she gazed into Trent's Caribbean blue eyes, she wondered just how far she'd let him go. Two buttons of her Marc Jacobs silk twill top were already unbuttoned and Trent was angling for a third. She almost let him, too, but—

"Stop, Trent! You know where this could lead."

Trent looked like he didn't know. "Where?"

"Someplace Jesus wouldn't like!" She searched her Très Jolie clutch for her rosary beads.

"Um, what?" said Trent, looking dreamy-adorable in a cinnamon Ted Baker polo, torn khaki shorts, and faded blue Vans. "Jesus doesn't approve of *second base*?"

"I'm pretty sure Jesus doesn't approve of *any* base,

Trent. And you know my pledge to him—and to the American TV-viewing public."

Trent looked like he didn't know. "Tell me again?"

"Trent?! It's to keep my legs crossed until I am joined in a holy union before God at, like, a church. With a big reception where I look really pretty. Then a honeymoon where I go to someplace really, totally amazing with my husband and then we do it, like, on the beach. For the first time. Ya know?"

Trent sucked his teeth. He didn't look happy. "But Tans, we've been going out a long time. We're even each other's dates for the Emmys. Doesn't that count for something in Jesus's eyes? I mean *at least* second base?"

Tanya sighed. Trent did have a point. But Tanya was pretty sure Jesus wouldn't go for second base—even if they were going to the Emmys together. "Why don't we get out of the car and kneel down and pray a little and ask him?"

"Forget it, Tans," said Trent, pulling away and adjusting his khaki shorts. "The praying thing is so lame. And the makeup dude has been really pissed at me lately because I have scabs on my knees from all the kneeling."

Tanya knew this had to be frustrating for Trent. She *also* knew his eyes weren't the only blue thing about him . . . but she couldn't help it. She had to hold off. Even though she sooooo wanted to be with Trent. "I understand, Trent," she said, buttoning up her top. "Why don't we just take a drive and, like, cool down?"

"Jeez, Tanya, you don't know how hard this is on a dude!" he exploded. "It's *very* hard!"

Tanya frowned. "Trent, as mad as you are at me, Tanya, the best and prettiest girlfriend you have ever had, you really shouldn't take the Lord's name in vain."

"Wha—? When? I didn't!"

"You said 'Jeez,' which everyone knows is Jesus's nickname. And I wish you wouldn't say it when you're angry."

"But that's when people say it! It's a word for when you're all, like, whoa, I don't know what else to say!" Trent was pouting. Tanya thought he looked so cute. She even wondered if she could reconsider the second base thing. She started to unbutton her blouse again, but immediately saw Jesus's face on the dashboard. She'd been having lots of Jesus visions lately, but in this one he looked really angry, staring at her from the odometer, so she quickly buttoned up her blouse.

Trent watched sadly as Tanya's boobs were declared off-limits. He then put the Cruiser in reverse and started down the canyon. As he maneuvered the bends and curves of Mulholland Drive, Tanya noticed the faraway look in his eyes—like he actually had something on his mind. This seemed strange to Tanya. She'd only ever seen Trent look like he had *nothing* on his mind. Except surfing. Or Little Debbies when he was having an anxiety attack.

"Thanks for understanding, Trent. I feel really comfortable with you. Like, really. Like, totally. Like, even, like—" Tanya stopped herself before she could say what she was about to say. Trent was looking over at her like, "Huh?" Her eyes began to well. Her heart rattled so loudly in her chest she thought for sure Trent could hear it. She'd almost just told Trent . . . *she loved him.*

"What's that look on your face?" said Trent, stealing

glances as he navigated the curvy canyon roads. "It's all, like, weird."

"Nothing, Trent," she said, covering. "Better keep your eye on the road. I mean *both* eyes. Not just one, which would be totally spastic." But Tanya knew she *couldn't* keep it in—the thing she was trying so hard not to say. It was pushing against the inside of her mouth like a little demon, a demon that wanted desperately to be exorcized—preferably by a Catholic priest. Or was it an angel inside trying to get out, one sent by Jesus? Or was it a demon disguised as an angel? Tanya's mind did backflips, but she couldn't stop that little demon/angel, no matter how hard she tried. "I LOVE YOU!" she finally cried.

Tanya clamped her eyes shut the minute the words were out. She felt as if the world had ended. It was completely silent as she held her breath. All she could hear was the purring of the engine and Trent's breathing. Her heart seemed to slow, then stop entirely. *Am I dead?* she thought.

"Tans?" Trent said, suddenly breathing so heavily he sounded like a psycho in one of those *Saw* movies. "I love you, too."

Tanya wasn't sure she heard right. Which wasn't a new sensation. She often felt she hadn't heard right. But then she realized: *I totally heard right* . . . "OHMYGOD," Tanya squealed, her eyes bursting open so hard she almost hurt herself. "THANK GOD YOU SAID IT BACK OR I WOULD HAVE FELT LIKE A TOTAL LOSER BUT I'M NOT, THANK GOD!"

Trent flinched. "Tans, you're, like, screaming at the top of your voice."

"OHMYGOD I KNOW IT'S JUST I'M SO EXCITED I'M, LIKE, CAUGHT IN LOUD MODE!"

Trent flinched again. "It's, like, *way* loud, Tans."

"I TOTALLY KNOW BECAUSE THE INSIDE OF MY HEAD IS LIKE, OW THAT'S SO LOUD!"

"Um, could you find a way to dial it down?"

Tanya took a few deep breaths. She looked out the window to get her bearings. They were driving west on Sunset Boulevard, passing Fresh, the salon where she had received her first exfoliating facial—the very first day she'd arrived in L.A. She took this as a sign that her and Trent's newly declared love was more than skin-deep. It was, in fact, pore-deep. She whispered a thank-you up to God, Jesus, and the Holy Spirit, and then turned to Trent, facing him for the first time since they'd spoken the words aloud.

"Trent, this is a magical night. You even look a little like a magician. And I feel like . . . your magician's assistant. Like, in a really tight outfit with thigh-high boots covered in sequins."

"I totally feel the same way, Tans. But reversed 'cause I don't want to wear those boots. But, yeah, like, there's magic in this car," he said, his baby blues looking to Tanya in this mind-blowing moment bluer than the bluest blue.

"Let's do something to always remember this night," she cooed. "Something special. Something only you and I—Trent Owen Michaels and Tanya Ventura—could do on a magical night like this."

Trent looked thoughtful for a full moment, which once again impressed Tanya, for whom thoughts were like icky, slippery eels trying to get away. "I got it," he said finally as he pulled into the parking lot in front of Jamba Juice. "Let's order two protein shakes with fiber boosts."

This wasn't exactly what Tanya had in mind. But she knew Trent wanted to keep in tip-top shape—and on his diet— while maintaining muscle mass, all of which she wanted to encourage. *Our physical beauty means the world to me—and to the American television audience, too,* she thought. Before the thought could leave her mind, she expressed it. "There's nothing I'd rather do, Trent, than keep fit and toned with you!"

## Malibu Beach—Max's Trailer—9:32 A.M., the Next Morning

The inside of Corliss's head felt as mushy as her mother's overcooked broccoli. She'd been interviewing nanny candidates for just over an hour, but so many had been disasters that Corliss was beginning to wonder if there was *any* appropriate child care in the greater Los Angeles area.

So far she'd interviewed a former gang member with a *killa* tattoo on her forehead, a bipolar nun with dyslexia, and a German bodybuilder who'd invited her to an all-nude weekend in Palm Desert. This one was sitting right in front of her, either winking repeatedly or working through a really bad tic. "Uh, no thanks on that nudie weekend invite," Corliss said, trying desperately to keep things in the professional realm. "I like to remain entirely clothed on weekends."

"Too bad," he said, then frowned and winked. "Is dat da end of da interview?"

"I think so," said Corliss, showing him to the door with the fake smile her uncle Ross had taught her. "And maybe you should get that tic checked out," she said under her breath. The bodybuilder-nanny frowned and stepped onto the beach. Once Corliss made sure he was all the way to the parking lot, she returned to her desk and plunked herself down in disbelief. "Thank God that's over. Jeez . . ."

Corliss was totally perplexed. All of the candidates had come highly recommended by Max's assistants, who sat a few feet away, diligently tap-tap-tapping away on their computers, perusing the various nanny sites Corliss had recommended. Could they possibly have thought those half-functioning outcasts would be suitable guardians for Legend?

Then it occurred to Corliss. Max's assistants didn't *want* her to find the perfect nanny for Legend. That's because Max's assistants didn't like Corliss! In fact, they probably wanted Corliss to fail in the nanny search—because they wanted her to fail at everything Max asked her to do. That's because all of them *wanted her job.*

"Everybody out!" Corliss bellowed when this realization hit her. She stood behind her desk with her hands on her hips, glad she'd worn the rather tailored Copines mini-jacket today because she felt it gave her more authority than she innately had. Of course her hair was a little listless because she'd tried a new conditioner, but she felt her tone of voice more than made up for her limp locks.

Max's assistants gave her that infuriating blank look they always gave her whenever she told them to do something.

"You heard me. The nanny search is over!" They kept giving her that blank look, the one they'd copied from Max. It was like staring at a sea of blank mini-Maxes. Finally, they turned their backs on Corliss and slouched insouciantly out of the trailer.

"God!" said Corliss, already spent and only two hours into her day. "It is so hard to get good help!"

"What did you say, Corliss . . . ?" It was Max, sticking his head in. "Or are you talking to yourself like I do?"

"I don't know *who* I'm talking to, Max. I'm so wrung out from interviewing nanny candidates. It's like all the psych wards up and down the coast suddenly went out of business and all the patients showed up here. Jeesh."

"I'm sorry to hear that, Corliss," said Max, paging through something on his iPhone. "But I absolutely need you to keep on it. I'm dealing with two impossible children at the moment and it's not easy."

"*Two* children?"

"Yes, Legend—and Anushka."

Corliss shook her head and braced herself for more bad Anushka news. "What now?"

Max sighed. "Well, we finally got her back into the bald cap and costume, but now she wants a henna tattoo in the shape of a fire-breathing dragon on top of her head. She says if we don't get her one she won't go before the cameras."

Corliss shook her head. "Yup, that sounds like Anushka . . . Can hair and makeup do the tattoo?"

"They just sent me a text saying they're working on it. I'm creatively visualizing that they'll have it on her willful little skull in a half hour so we won't lose any more time. We're shooting on location in a fabulous mansion today and we've got to get the cast moving. Meanwhile, Legend is doing everything he can to undo the effects of the two anxiety pills I took with my midmorning snack . . ."

Max looked like a little boy lost in the woods. It was a look that Corliss had seen before—one she could never resist. But she held her tongue. *Professionalism* was going to be her watchword from this point forward and she simply wasn't going to be taken in by the need to take care of Max. No matter how cute and little-boy-lost he looked.

"Please, Corliss," he continued. "It's *imperative* you find a nanny for Legend. I can't start filming the third episode unless I'm in my clear zone. Which, as you recall, is a zone where everything goes away and all that's left is *me*."

"Okay, Max," said Corliss, sighing. She knew Max's advanced narcissism was his only weapon against the world. She also knew it was her duty to protect it at all costs, especially during production—so professionalism had to meet caretakerism. She turned to her computer to search for more nanny websites. "I'll do my best."

"Thank you, Corliss. I know you'll find someone fabulous. Do you want my assistants to keep helping?"

"Absolutely not!"

## Estate Overlooking Malibu—10:37 A.M.

Rihanna had listed the property with the most exclusive

real estate agent in Malibu. While it was on the market, *The 'Bu* had rented the spectacular home to shoot the opening scene of the third episode. Michael Rothstein had decreed that he wanted the opening scene of this episode to have "wow appeal." The house certainly had it—especially the room Max and the cast found themselves in.

The blue stone fireplace was two stories high. A Murano glass chandelier dripped thousands of glittering red shards from a height of thirty feet. Windows soared to the top of a vaulted ceiling where teak Tibetan beams crisscrossed in a tangle of intricately carved artistry.

Except for Anushka, who was in another bathing suit, the cast was assembled in their evening glamwear—which meant more clothes than usual. They were posed against an ancient Belgian tapestry that covered one entire wall. Twenty grips scurried around them, adjusting the lights to make their beautiful faces glow just so. The grips were having trouble lighting Tanya, however, because she was wearing a black hooded bathrobe and her face was covered in Dead Sea mud. "Max?" she said, raising her hand as the technicians fluttered about her, hitting her with more and more wattage.

"Yes, Tanya," said Max, praying that she wasn't about to ask one of her patented dum-dum questions. "What is it?"

"Because there's all this light on me, my mud mask is, like, becoming caked to my face. Which is making my face all itchy. Like, totally itchy. Like, *ow* itchy."

Trent beamed at her, his eyes blazing. His mouth hung open even more than it usually did. She gazed back at him, the mud around her mouth cracking as she smiled too big. It was clear to everyone they were once again madly in love—inseparable and insufferable.

"Patience, Tanya," said Max. "Actresses all over Hollywood have sacrificed more for their art than a little itch. Creatively visualize that your face is floating above everything, peaceful and free from the rest of your body."

Tanya scrunched up what she could of her face. "But then wouldn't I be beheaded?"

"Um—" said Max, who was immediately distracted by Legend tugging at his Zegna cotton check pants. "What is it now, Legend?"

"Can you take me to the little boyth room?" he asked at the top of his voice.

"I mean," said Tanya, plowing on, "if I was beheaded I couldn't talk and say my lines. Right?"

"Tanya," said Max, "I didn't say you were *beheaded*. I said you should creatively visualize—"

"Max," Anushka interrupted from across the room. "I want the light to hit my right side where the henna tattoo is. This dude"—she pointed at one of the grips—"is lighting my left side."

"Light Anushka's right side, please," said Max to the grip as his eye began to twitch. Anushka turned her head to better show off her tattoo. The grip did as he was told.

Legend once again tugged on Max's pants. "Boyth room, boyth room!"

"Okay, Legend," whispered Max, trying to keep it together,

and wondering desperately how Corliss was doing on the nanny search. "But didn't you just go to the boyth—I mean boys—room?"

"That wath for number one," Legend shouted, even louder than before. "Now I hafta do a big poop."

The cast giggled. Max went red. "Legend," he said, bending down and lowering his voice further. "That's not a word we say when we're not at home."

"Thorry."

"JB," said Max, "would you mind taking Legend to the bathroom? You're not in the first part of this scene and I'm almost in my clear space."

"Sure thing," said JB, finishing a series of sit-ups. He'd been furiously pumping his once scrawny, now slightly less scrawny muscles all morning as the technicians had been setting up. He got to his feet, then lifted his bony little arms in the air. Two enormous semicircles of sweat clung to his pits. "Uh-oh, Max, I think the Jeebster needs to change shirts again . . ."

Max sighed and looked around for the costume crew. "JB, why do you insist on getting all sweaty before we shoot? This is the second time this morning we've had to pull you another shirt because of your overactive endocrine system."

"Sorry, Max," said JB, hopping from foot to foot. "Just trying to keep myself busy. Put the ol' excess energy to good use—if you know what I mean. Wouldn't you rather have me working out my poppin' bod than sinking all my moolah into bad stock trades and giving the blogosphere more bad publicity ammunition?" He smiled impishly.

Before Max could reply, Legend tugged at his pants again. "I really have to poop!" the shrunken preschooler yelled.

"Yes," said Max, rubbing his temples, "we all got that particular news flash, Legend. JB, can you please take your stinky pits and my stepbrother to the restroom?"

"Aye, aye, Captain," said JB, saluting. He took Legend by the hand and they scampered off down a hallway. Max texted Corliss: NANNY SEARCH???

Anushka was cracking up. "Gotta love a kid who screams 'poop.'"

One of the grips shot Max a look. "Anushka, can you *please* keep still while they light you?"

"Max," said Rocco, approaching. He looked incredibly fit after his rehab stint in Sicily.

"Yes, what is it, Rocco?" said Max, backing up a little as he did whenever Rocco came his way.

"I'm genuinely looking forward to today's shoot. The writing on this episode is a lot stronger than usual. Better character development, more innovative plot twists . . . It's quite an improvement."

"Thank you, Rocco," said Max, who felt a bit confused; he was so much more used to Rocco giving him attitude than praise. In fact, Rocco still totally intimidated Max. Rocco was wicked smart, hyperarticulate, built like a wall of bricks—and related to the famous Bellucci family. Four things Max was not. "I'm glad you're looking so well, by the way, Rocco. I've got a few ideas about how we're going to shoot this scene. I know you're interested in directing someday, so maybe you'll learn a little something."

"I'm sure I will, Max," said Rocco with an out-of-character humility. "And let me add I'm greatly looking forward to hearing your ideas." He bowed a little in Max's direction.

"Thank you, Rocco," Max said, bowing back a little. He knew he had to play it cool to keep Rocco's respect, but inside his stomach crumpled. The truth was, Max had zero ideas about how to shoot the scene. He was going to wing it like he always did.

A cold sweat broke out on his forehead as he was once again reminded just how giant a fake he was. He went to bite his cuticles, but then he realized he'd spent four hundred dollars on them the day before, so he signaled one of his assistants to bring him a bowl of wasabi peas instead. The assistant ran off and Corliss ran up.

"Corliss! Has there been any luck with the nanny search? Legend is so up in my grill I need a—a—"

"Grill protector?"

"Something like that, yes."

"Well, I did just get a lead on an *amazing* nanny who comes highly recommended from the Scientology Celebrity Centre International. I'm just waiting for a call back from her agent."

Max was overjoyed. "A nanny with an agent? Endorsed by L. Ron Hubbard? She sounds perfect!"

"Fingers crossed," said Corliss. "While I'm waiting for the call, do you mind if I hang out and watch the scene?"

"Not at all, you know your presence is usually a comfort to me."

"Thanks. I think . . ."

"Okay, people," Max said, seeing that the grips had finally bathed the cast in a perfectly golden otherworldly glow. "Let's have a look at you." They looked, in a word, dazzling. Especially Anushka. Bald and hennaed, she cut a striking figure in an off-the-shoulder Michael Kors midnight black cocktail dress. Lately she'd been looking less and less like America's Naughty Sweetheart, and more and more like a sophisticated woman of the world.

"Anushka," said Max, marveling at her transformation, "I hope you don't take this the wrong way, but someone should have put you in a bald cap a long time ago. You look simply amazing."

"Right?" she said. "I am *owning* this chrome dome!"

"It looks so good on you, you might even consider going hairless to the Emmys," said Max, circling her approvingly.

"Uh, don't think so, Max—but good try. I'm featuring full hairification for the Emmys, thank you very much."

"That reminds me, people," said Max, consulting the tickler file on his iPhone. "Everyone needs to submit the name of their Emmy date to Michael Rothstein's office by Friday for security clearance."

"I submit Trent!" yelped Tanya.

"And I submit her," said Trent, pointing deliriously at Tanya.

"Ha!" said Anushka. "Big surprise. As for little ol' bald me, I'm probably going to bring that pretty stoner model Tyler. He's always good for a few laughs."

"I'm bringing my cousin Patrizio," said Rocco, "who will be visiting from Italy. He's fascinated by American pop culture, so the evening should be interesting for him."

"JB?" said Max. "Have you asked someone yet?"

"Me?" said JB, looking helpless. "Good one! Naw, no girly yet. How's 'bout you, Cor? You figured out who you're going to ask?"

"Jeez, no," she said, "I'm still getting over the shock of being invited."

Was it Max's imagination or was Corliss batting her eyelashes at JB?

"Okay," Max said, banishing the thought from his head as he saw that the camerawoman was ready. "We'll begin momentarily, but an announcement before we do. I have decreed, with the support of the front office, that there is to be *no dating* among anyone involved in the production of *The 'Bu*." Tanya opened her mouth to protest, but Max cut her off before she had the chance. "Tanya, you and Trent got in under the wire. There's nothing we can do about your, er, relationship now."

"Thanks, Max!" she said, clapping.

"But everyone else will have to look *elsewhere* for any romance. It's too disruptive and potentially damaging to morale to date the people you work with. Do we all understand one another?"

Everyone nodded—except for Anushka, who exploded in her signature, "Ha!"

"What is it, Anushka? Will this rule be hard for you to comply with?"

"Uh, don't worry, Max. There's a *total* lack of sexual tension among this group, that's for sure."

"Exactly what I want to hear," said Max. "Now please get in your places. We're ready to shoot. I want you to put yourself in the emotional states of these characters. Anushka's character Alecia has survived the Malibu Canyon fire, recovered from amnesia, and just returned from an ashram in Mumbai to find her parents have been killed in a plane crash. The rest of you are here to comfort her and encourage her to go on with her life."

The cast nodded thoughtfully. The camerawoman took her place behind the camera. The sound was rolling. The slate was prepped.

Max still had absolutely no idea how the scene would go. So he did the only thing he knew how to do: He creatively visualized general fabulousness and called out, "*Action!*"

# ★ The 'Bu

## Script Insert #1

INT. A PALATIAL ESTATE HIGH IN THE CANYON

ALECIA, her grief on gorgeous display in a
drop-dead black cocktail dress, lounges on
a gold brocade CHAISE. Her eyes are puffy
from weeping. She looks wan and helpless. As
the surf crashes beneath her family's MALIBU
VILLA, she gazes into the distance.

                    A VOICE
          Alecia . . . ?

She turns to find TRAVIS and RAMONE coming
into the sunken living room.

                    ALECIA
          You're here!

                    RAMONE
          Of course. Our differences are
          all in the past.

                    ALECIA
        And Travis . . . ? It's beautiful
        out, the surf's high—you gave that
        up to visit me?

                    TRAVIS
        Yeah.


Travis moves toward her. Alecia covers her
head.


                    ALECIA
        But I don't want you to see me
        like this . . .


                    TRAVIS
        It doesn't matter, Alecia . . .
        you're alive.


                    RAMONE
        And we're all friends . . . that's
        *all* that matters.


A FIGURE IN A DARK ROBE enters the room.
Alecia cowers.


                    ALECIA
        Ahh!

THE FIGURE

Don't be scared. It's me—Tessa.
(She kneels at Alecia's side.)
I've been upstairs, staying here
in the house this whole time,
looking out for you. Waiting
until you were strong enough to
face the world again. I guess
all the stress—the fire, what's
happened to you—has worn me
down. I put on this robe because
I think I may have caught a
chill . . .

Alecia searches their faces for the
antagonism they'd all felt for her just
before the fire—but she doesn't find it.

ALECIA

Looking out for me? Putting your
health in danger because you're
worried . . . about me? It's
unbelievable. I really do have
friends!

END OF SCENE.

# Three

"What is it, my darling?" asked Uncle Ross as he searched the depths of his fridge for a missing jar of olives. "I haven't seen you this blue since I told you it wasn't a good idea to wear stripes with plaid."

Corliss sighed as she prepared Uncle Ross's third martini. She was spent. Beat. Wiped out. The last thing she needed was Uncle Ross's sarcasm. Her day had been filled with Legend's nanny search—and by the end of it there was still no nanny in sight. "I'm just really down in the proverbial dumps, Uncle Ross. I mean, I deferred a full scholarship to study psychology—at Columbia University, no less!—to work in television. *Television!*"

"Isn't that what you're doing?" Uncle Ross replied, finding the jar of olives behind some leftover diver scallops from the Hungry Cat.

"No! That is exactly *not* what I am doing, Uncle Ross.

What I'm doing is interviewing ex-cons and debilitated members of society to see if they want to be Legend's nanny!" She was so riled up she was shaking Uncle Ross's martini furiously.

Uncle Ross frowned and rescued the martini shaker from Corliss. "Dearest niece, I asked you to shake my martini, not choke it to death." He poured the martini out, plunked two plump olives in the liquid, and took a long sip. "Ah, my evening is now complete."

Corliss shook her head and threw her hands in the air. "Uncle Ross, you're impossible. You think the answer to all life's problems can be found in the perfect martini!" She stormed out of the room.

"Excuse me, where are you going, young lady?"

"I'm giving up," she called from down the hall. "I'm going to take to my bed with a stack of *CosmoGirls*, regret every decision I've made in my life, and maybe come down in an hour to eat a pint of Chunky Monkey."

"Corliss, that sounds like a terrible idea. Especially when I just had the Bentley detailed." Uncle Ross smiled his devilish smile. The one that said, *Let's be naughty.*

Uncle Ross's Bentley was the most gorgeous car Corliss had ever seen: cream-colored with a classic chrome grill and a sinfully soft buttermilk leather interior. It was only taken out for the specialest of special occasions, and Corliss had been allowed to ride in it exactly once—when Uncle Ross had taken her to see Justin Timberlake in concert at the Staples Center. "What do you say, Corliss? She's sitting out front. We can hit Beverly Hills, window-shop for things only rich people like me can afford, then get a Kobe steak at that fabulous restaurant Cut?"

Corliss's eyes opened wide. She hadn't had an "Uncle Ross" date in weeks. She was supposed to read over the latest 'Bu draft and tell Max what was in it first thing tomorrow morning, but she thought a night on the town might do her a world of good . . . change up her attitude. Which is exactly what she needed. She couldn't help but smile a naughty smile back. "Uncle Ross, you totally know how to fly with style."

"Is that a yes?" he said with a hopeful look as he downed the dregs of his martini and dangled the keys of the Bentley in front of her.

"Is this the face of a girl saying no?" said Corliss as she reached for the keys to the Bentley.

## Beverly Hills—Wolfgang Puck's Cut—8:45 P.M.

Corliss beheld the sleek Richard Meier interior in awe. The curved wall of windows that looked out to the Beverly Wilshire Hotel. The long blond teak bar. The soaring ceiling. And the celebrities! Across the room Leighton Meester was digging into a sirloin the size of her head. To Leighton's left were Victoria and David Beckham, feeding each other Austrian oxtail. Inches from the stunning couple sat Eva Mendes, polishing off a porterhouse. Corliss had had some glam experiences since arriving in L.A., but sitting in this white-hot restaurant watching big stars chow down on cow ranked at the very top of the list.

"Corliss," said Uncle Ross, perusing the menu, "shall we

order the bone marrow flan as an appetizer?"

"What?!" Corliss was not about to eat anything that had the words *bone* or *marrow* in it. Especially if the word *flan* was anywhere nearby. "Um, I think I'll pass, Uncle Ross. You keep forgetting, I'm kind of a meat and potatoes girl."

Uncle Ross wagged his finger. "Corliss, when in Rome..."

*No way*, thought Corliss, who was still recovering from the strange poached egg pizza he'd made her eat at Mozza. "Yes, Uncle Ross, but we're not in Rome. This is Beverly Hills, remember? What about a good old-fashioned sirloin? Trimmed of fat, of course. I'm still trying to get down to my fighting weight." She momentarily put down the breadstick she'd been chomping on. She didn't want to look less than chic in this place—especially with all the superskinny women slathered in bling and couture sitting near her.

"Corliss, there's nothing wrong with your weight. Besides, you look adorable lately. You've somehow managed to combine a kind of down-market Indiana chic with a kind of up-and-coming west coast aplomb."

"Thanks, Uncle Ross!" she said, beaming at one of his rare—if not backhanded—compliments. "I knew there was a reason I accepted this date with you."

Uncle Ross cleared his throat. "Which reminds me, Corliss. Just exactly *when* is the last time my adorable, accomplished niece had a date."

Corliss immediately grabbed three breadsticks and crammed them in her mouth. "You know what? Maybe we should order that bloody bone pudding thingy," she said, trying to get off the dreaded dating topic. "Bone and blood is always a good combination," she continued, hearing how ridiculous she sounded but unable to stop her babble. "I mean, two great tastes that go great together, right? And then there's the pudding aspect, which sounds so yummy and—"

"Corliss," said Uncle Ross, leaning in to whisper, "you're blathering. Is dating a topic you'd rather not discuss?"

"No, not at all," she said, trying to swallow a mouthful of bread carbs. "But what's to discuss? Everyone dates, you win some, you lose some, blah, blah—dating, right?"

"Corliss, this is Uncle Ross you're talking to. I understand all. Which is how I've been able to put up with Jurgen's shenanigans all these years. You don't have to be evasive around me. I have a sense it's been a rather long time since you've had a proper date. Is that right?"

Uncle Ross was practically licking his lips. Corliss had to be careful. She knew whatever info she conveyed to him about her personal life might come back to haunt her later. The fact was—she'd *never* been on a date. Ever. In her whole life. And while she was just *dying* to unload about all of this to *someone*, she was reluctant to choose loose-lips Uncle Ross. "Come on," he said, devilishly. "If you can't trust your relatives . . ."

Corliss was so tempted. Her quandary was not something she could discuss with, for instance, Anushka—she'd just laugh. Max, of course, was out for professional reasons. And the only other prominent person in her life at the moment was Legend, the nannyless pygmy.

Corliss sighed and decided—against her better judgment—that honesty was the best policy. She'd give Uncle Ross a chance. Maybe he might be able to help her, even. And with the Emmys coming up, she needed all the help she could get. The thought of going dateless to that event was too painful to bear.

"Uncle Ross, your niece, Corliss Meyers, the girl who sits before you, has a big secret."

Uncle Ross nearly leaped out of his seat. He *lived* for secrets.

She motioned for him to sit back down. Victoria Beckham was giving him a weird look. "Calm down, Uncle Ross. It's a secret you're *not* going to like. The truth is . . . I've never had a date. Not ever. Not in Indiana-no-place and not in Hollyweird. Not here, not there, and in all likelihood, not to the Emmys, either. There, I said it." She felt a wave of relief once it was out in the open.

Uncle Ross responded with the strangest look. He cocked his head right, then left. Then right, then left, then right, then left, really fast. "Corliss, I'm—I'm—I'm—cocking my head . . ."

"I can see that, Uncle Ross. Are you okay? Maybe you have a brain disorder? Something neurological?"

"Corliss, no, it's not my brain. It's your confession! It—it can't be true . . . What's happened to you? *Never* had a date? That's like saying you've never taken a breath, drunk a glass of water, peed standing up!"

"Um—"

"Sorry—take back that last one. But never a date?!

And you're considering going to the Emmys *stag*? How can this catastrophe be happening to us?" He slumped in his chair like one of her mother's overcooked carrots.

"To *us*, Uncle Ross? I kinda think my lack of a dating life has really nothing to do with you."

"But it does! It brings our entire family's dating juju way, way down. I mean, I'm lucky I'm in a relationship—but you never know what life holds in store for me down the road."

"Um—weren't we talking about *me*?"

"I mean," he plowed on, "what if I one day find myself single again—and afflicted with whatever it is *you* have?" Uncle Ross clutched the piping of his Evan Pique polo and swooned. "We absolutely have to fix this, Corliss. Ideally before we order dinner . . ."

"Too late," said Corliss, hugely relieved as the waiter arrived in a starched white apron and spiky black hair. She smiled up at him, trying to pretend everything was okay. "I'll have the twenty-one-day-aged rib eye and my uncle will have the pink Nebraskan sirloin." The waiter nodded and went away.

"Corliss, I don't know how I'm going to eat . . ."

"You know what, Uncle Ross?" said Corliss, now completely regretting ever embarking on a conversation about her absent love life. "I'm not so hungry myself." The fact was, she suddenly felt so sad. What *was* she afflicted with? Would she ever be like the other girls? Sure, she'd managed to pull *some* kind of acceptable look together since coming to L.A. She'd also wrestled her skin condition to the ground, got some very flattering highlights, and the occasional pumpkin-colored tan. She was, in fact, looking pretty good! Still, she remained dateless and *would* remain dateless on one of Hollywood's biggest nights—unless something happened soon. The thought cut into her like a steak knife.

She folded her hands in her lap. "Would you be really upset with me if we just went home, Uncle Ross? This place is great, but I've got a lot of reading to do for Max."

Uncle Ross frowned and nodded. "I understand, Corliss."

## Beverly Hills—The Sidewalk Outside Harry Winston Jewelers— Ten Minutes Later

Corliss and Uncle Ross peered through the glass windows of the closed store. The awkwardness of their restaurant conversation had completely evaporated in the face of the spectacular case of diamond necklaces they beheld just beyond their reach. "I can't believe people actually *touch* those things," said Corliss, "let alone wear them around their necks!" Uncle Ross rapped his knuckle on the glass door. Corliss laughed. "As if they'd let us in after closing time . . . you're too much, Uncle Ross."

A devastating blond gentleman in a crisp Armani three-button suit appeared inside the store and opened the door. "Mr. Meyers," he said in the smoothest man-voice Corliss had ever heard. "Thank you for calling ahead." He waved them in. Corliss looked back and forth between the two men in astonishment.

"Thank *you*, Jeremy," said Uncle Ross with a wink. "And you're looking very snappy, I might add." Jeremy made a slight, appreciative bow, then vanished.

Corliss stood in silent awe for a full moment. "Uncle Ross, being with you is like watching Matt Damon in *The Bourne Trilogy*: I never know what's coming next."

"What can I say?" He shrugged and moved to a display case. "I have ex-lovers in high places."

Corliss joined him to see what he was looking at. "What are we doing here, Uncle Ross . . . ?"

"We are at the ultimate jewelers, Corliss, looking at the best jewels in the world. Kings, queens, presidents—and the ladies of *The View*—have come through this door. As for what we are *doing* here . . . take a look at this a moment." He pointed at an exquisite blue diamond set in delicate white gold. The gem seemed to hover above its setting, like something from an ethereal realm.

Corliss was entranced, bewitched, bedazzled. "That's the most beautiful engagement ring I've ever seen in my total entire life, Uncle Ross."

"Exactly, Corliss," he said, giving her a level look. "And wouldn't you like to have one of those on your hand one day?"

*Now* Corliss knew what they were doing here. Uncle Ross was going to shame her into talking about her lonely life. His tactics sometimes made her so mad! She decided to hit him where he lived—the great generational divide that existed between them. "Uncle Ross, I don't mean to play the age card, but women of my generation have zero interest in being seduced by diamonds given to them by prospective husbands. First of all, we know these gems are quarried by underpaid South African workers and we protest that!"

"Listen to Little Miss Liberal," Uncle Ross said, moving to look at other diamond rings. "Corliss, I'm not saying you have to possess a sixty-karat brilliant cut with tons of gem fire to declare your worthiness as a woman, I'm just saying you *might maybe* want to get married someday. And to get married you need a fiancé. And to get a fiancé you have to—last time I checked—have a boyfriend. And to have a boyfriend you have to go on a freakin' date!" Uncle Ross never raised his voice like this. Or said the word *freakin'*. "Sorry, Corliss, I'm all worked up. You've shaken me to the core. We really have to fix this situation you're in."

Corliss looked to the heavens and wished she prayed, because if she did, she'd pray to God to shut Uncle Ross up about her love life.

"Can I be of help?" said Jeremy, silently appearing at the display case.

"Yes," said Corliss. "You can help see us out, thank you." With that she turned on her heels and left the store.

## Uncle Ross's Bentley—Five Minutes Later

Uncle Ross drove in silence. Corliss wasn't about to break it. She knew he was right: It was high time she dove into the dating pool. But she didn't know how to swim! The whole idea of dating was what initially kicked her skin condition into high gear junior year of high school. The thought of small talk, flirting, and splitting the check threw her into a hives tailspin. But she also knew being a dateless wonder in Indiana-no-place was one thing and being a dateless wonder in Los Angeles on Emmy night was a catastrophe that bordered on the pathetic.

"Okay, okay, okay!" she finally blurted. "I'll admit it. I'm a total social loser! I'm eighteen years old, my skin finally cleared up, and I live in Los Angeles—where people are dating left, right, and center. I need to start dating, too—you're right, Uncle Ross. Even though I kinda hate you right now because you're right."

Uncle Ross let out a huge sigh. "Thank God you hate me because I'm right, Corliss. Because I *am* right. Now what are we going to do about it? Are there any dating candidates in your life? Boys with money, power, and their own Italian tailor? You have to aim high, Corliss."

"Slow down there, Uncle Ross. Let's just start with someone who might ask me out!"

Uncle Ross made a sharp turn onto Sunset Boulevard. Corliss gripped the dashboard. "Corliss, please! You can't sit around waiting for *them* to ask *you* out! That's probably what got you into this awful mess in the first place!"

"Um," said Corliss, increasingly scared by Uncle Ross's passion. "I think you're a little over-invested here?"

"Corliss," said Uncle Ross, taking on his very serious voice. "Listen to me, this town is brutal. If you haven't been married at least once by the time you're twenty-five, you're sunk in the eyes of everyone. Unless, of course, you're gay like me. Then you just need to have a big house by the time you're twenty-five."

"I can assure you, Uncle Ross, I'm not gay like you. Or

like anybody. And there are no prospective dating candidates in my life." The minute she said this she knew she was lying. There was JB. While not exactly a great prospective *dating* candidate, he was looking pretty great lately. When he wasn't on set he didn't wear his glasses—thanks to a recent LASIK surgery. Turns out he had really pretty green eyes. Also, little tiny muscles were beginning to form where a normal boy's pecs would be. The push-ups he'd been doing to keep his mind off day-trading were beginning to pay off.

"What is it, Corliss? You look thoughtful, and that always worries me."

"I was just thinking how JB looks almost normal now that he doesn't have to wear his retainer . . ." she said dreamily, forgetting that Uncle Ross was there. She was lost in a little JB reverie, which had happened a few times this week.

"Aha!" said Uncle Ross, "so there *is* someone! This is that JB from the show? The one with the goofy Jack Purcell sneakers and the sunken chest?"

Corliss couldn't help but blush. She was caught. "It's not so sunken anymore, Uncle Ross. He's been exercising."

"Perfect! He has a job, he takes care of himself, he's not so gorgeous that you have to worry around other girls, but he's kind of cute in that kind-of-cute-if-you-squint-really-hard way. I say you ask him out," he concluded decisively.

Corliss went white. The thought of such a thing made her stomach fall to her knees. She turned her head so Uncle Ross couldn't see. Outside, the mansions of Sunset Boulevard flashed by.

"Corliss, I've had a lot of experience with men. You have to chase him—but with discretion. So he doesn't know he's being chased."

"But how do I do that, Uncle Ross? When it comes to all that stuff I'm completely developmentally impaired."

"How you do it is by inviting him to something that doesn't seem like a date-date. Something like a party or event, preferably where some of your friends are. So it just looks like what you kids call 'hanging out.' Then you act delightful and wear something low cut and he realizes he should ask *you* to something. Next thing you know you're getting an engagement ring and losing your virginity—not necessarily in that order."

Corliss laughed. She couldn't imagine JB being responsible for either event. But she did think Uncle Ross's suggestion wasn't bad.

"You look thoughtful again, Corliss," he said, turning into his driveway.

"Well," she said, the wheels turning in her head as she contemplated her uncle's advice. "The Emmy Awards are coming up. Everyone on the show has been invited. Max even swung two tickets for me as a kind of thanks for all my hard work. I guess I could suggest to JB that we go together . . ."

"Of course you could," Uncle Ross purred. "You'd both be there, anyway. Call him *tonight*."

"Tonight?!" Corliss was terrified.

"Yes, Corliss Meyers, you'll do as I say. In the meantime I'll ring Donatella in Milan and see if she has any samples she can lend us. Something flawless for my favorite niece."

"You know Donatella Versace?!"

"DV and I were squash partners in the 80s. That woman has a backhand that could catapult you into the middle of next week. Now don't worry about any of this, Corliss. I have a master plan—and I never fail when it comes to matters of the heart."

Corliss gulped and saw the evening of the Emmys in front of her like a vision. She was in Versace, JB was in . . . something not too offensive. They laughed and cuddled and finally kissed. But even in the vision she felt like a dork, all fake and awkward. She wanted to leap from the car and run screaming into the night. But it was pitch-black out and Uncle Ross's driveway was a mile long, so she worried about finding her way home.

## The Sunset Tower—Anushka's Penthouse Apartment—10:42 P.M.

"You're flipping the channels too fast!" yelped Tanya.

Anushka was indeed flipping the channels too fast. *Dancing with the Stars*, *Project Runway*, and *Desperate Housewives* (she'd TiVoed them all) flew by at the speed of light. "It all sucks butt, anyway," Anushka finally replied. "*Desperate Housewhatevers!* I mean, all those strung-out old ladies on one block? And *Dancing with the Farts*? All those ancient stars trying to kick their faces? Can't all of them retire like *normal* old people?" She was curled up on her chaise, wrapped in a cashmere throw, scowling at the five-foot square flat-screen TV.

"Anushka, that's a terrible thing to say," reprimanded Tanya. "How can they retire when they probably need money for their arthritis medicine?"

Anushka rolled her eyes, threw down the remote, and moved to the floor-to-ceiling window that looked out over Los Angeles, which shimmered and spread out before her. Once there she sighed heavily at the tragedy of her life. It was bad enough she was playing a bald burn victim on national TV, but now she had to endure an evening with Tanya, the cortex-impaired fashion model.

"Hey!" Tanya chirped. "We could watch *The 'Bu* pilot. I haven't seen it in a while . . ."

"You mean the one where I die a fiery death? No, thank you." Tanya was now *really* bugging Anushka. Of course, she always bugged her a little, but tonight she was bugging her in great big chunks. She'd only called her over because Corliss had been *completely and totally* bugging her lately by towing the Max party line. Anushka liked things so much better when Corliss was entirely on *her* side and they could trash Max behind his back all they wanted. But lately she was all "Max this" and "Max that" and "I Have So Much Responsibility!" It made Anushka want to barf.

"All I know," continued Tanya, oblivious to Anushka's dark mood, "is that Jesus loves old people just as much as young people. Maybe even more because they are closer to dying—which means he'll see them soon." Tanya twirled her chocolate brown locks and looked vacantly at the ceiling.

Anushka rolled her eyes again. She really should have called Corliss. "Tans, take it way down on the Jesus chatter, 'kay? Don't get me wrong—he's great and all—but these days I'm a little like, 'What have you done for me lately, dude?'"

*Especially in the love department,* was what she was thinking. The truth was, Anushka was lonely. She was just glad Tanya wasn't babbling on about Trent like usual.

Tanya nodded sympathetically. "I know what you mean. Jesus makes me crazy sometimes! He wants you to have love in your life, right? But then you meet a gorgeous guy like Trent and you're all, like, hot, and Jesus steps in and says, *Whoa, you can't have sex!* I mean, what's the deal, Jesus?"

"See, that's just it, Tans," Anushka said through her teeth, turning from the window and balling her fists in frustration. "I don't *have* a boyfriend at the moment—if you haven't noticed. That's why I'm here watching TV with a *girlfriend.*"

"Oh," said Tanya, who looked as if it were finally sinking in. "I wondered why you called me to come over."

"I'm sorry," Anushka sighed, plunking herself down on the floor next to Tanya. "I'm just totally cranky because my romantic life is in the dumpster! Also, I'm totally PMSing."

"Wow," said Tanya, looking suddenly perplexed. "I never knew you had real feelings like other girls . . ."

"What?!" shrieked Anushka.

"Oops, that came out wrong . . ." Tanya scrunched up her face in the way she did whenever she needed to activate her brain. "What I meant to say was that you—the totally amazing Anushka Peters—never seem like you need a boyfriend. You're, like, totally independent."

This made Anushka really sad. She got a little teary, in fact. Of course she needed a boyfriend! She usually had at least one, in fact. But she didn't know what was wrong with her lately.

Every time she approached a guy he'd head for the Hollywood Hills. Or worse, he'd be all over her like Hayden Panettiere in a kissing booth.

"The thing is, Tans, I *totally* need a guy. At least to take to the Emmys. I was planning on asking Tyler, but he's always sneaking off and then coming back with the munchies. It's gross—and embarrassing. Even for me. Ha!" But her laughter faded as she once again realized the gravity of her singleness. "You have Trent and I have . . . no one."

Tanya made the biggest pouty-face possible. "You don't have a date for the Emmys! That is completely the suckiest thing I've ever heard. What can I do to help? Get Trent to fix you up with one of his surf buddies?"

"No, thank you," said Anushka. "Anushka Peters doesn't do surfers anymore. It takes weeks to get the sand out of the backseat of my car. I'm just going to have to figure it out for myself—as usual." Somehow knowing this made her mood brighten. That's because self-reliance was the only reliance Anushka knew. "Besides, tonight there's only one thing to do: turn the TV back on and watch a lot of old ladies get laid by the wrong guys. HA!"

And so they turned the TV back on. Anushka even leaned her head against Tanya's shoulder. *Tanya isn't about to solve global warming anytime soon, but at least,* Anushka thought, *she is* here.

**Somewhere Over the Rainbow—11:12 P.M.**

# ¡The Bu-Hoo

*'Bu*-nanas—

It is with a heavy heart that I report that Anushka "Champagne Breath" Peters and Max Marx, aka M2, are already at each other's throats. Again. Can't these two get along? Isn't it time they grew up and did their jobs? It breaks my heart to report such strife!

**KIDDING!** *I LOVES IT!*

First her eyebrows were all over the map, then her head got bald. B-ald! ROFL! (You'll believe it when you sees it ;)p) These two are testing each other in a big way. This is a showdown, *'Bu* babies, and only one of these raging egomaniacs will get out alive!

**CUE: AUDIENCE CHEERS**

Of course, they'll make nicey-nice for the Emmys. Our 'Bu stars can't be *nominated* this year—the show hasn't been on long enough—but they are invited. Expect the whole crew to show up dressed to the boobies (man boobies and otherwise) in schwag they haven't paid for!

## PAGING STELLA MCCARTNEY! PAGING ALEXANDER MCQUEEN!

But the *muy, muy importante* question is who will they bring??? That's where the fun comes in.

Word up and down Sunset Boulevard is Champagne Breath might fly solo this year—YIKES!—while Trent and Tanya will be sitting on each other's laps—NATCH—while Rocco DiSteroids is going bachelor style with his cousin from Italy—fly that red and green flag!

I hear even Little Miss Corliss "Clueless" Meyers has got her newly manicured hands on *a pair* of tickets. Whoa, Momma! Who's our Midwestern Mess gonna tumble into the Shrine Auditorium with????

Love is in the air, my peeps, make no mistake about it! And soon it's going to play itself out on the red carpet. And guess who will be there to bring you the backstage 411? You know who, dontcha?

MBK! For reals!

Yours in total 'Bu-ness,
MBK

### Uncle Ross's House—Corliss's Bedroom—11:37 P.M.

Corliss sat on her bed, hugging her knees for dear life. She stared at her phone, which seemed to taunt her from the top of her comforter, shifting shapes, sneering at her, sticking its tongue out. She closed her eyes tight and rocked back and forth, humming to herself like a crazy person . . .

She didn't know why it was so hard! She was only trying to follow Uncle Ross's directions to call up JB and invite him to the Emmys—and pretend it was just "hanging out" with the gang.

But it wasn't working. She'd been staring at the phone for a half hour, her eyes growing bigger each minute. They were currently the size of two beer coasters. Then it occurred to her: She should just rehearse her lines like the actors on *The 'Bu* rehearsed theirs. She would imagine herself *playing a scene with JB* and that's how she'd get through this.

"Hey, JB," she said, reciting from a script she was simultaneously writing in her head. "It's me, your coworker Corliss Meyers. I was just sitting around thinking, you know, about the Emmys and how it would be fun if we went together as just, um, two coworkers just having a good coworking time." She let the sentence hang in the air to see how she felt about it. "Blah!" She screamed after deciding she felt completely vomitous about it.

She threw herself facedown on the bed. "I can't do it!" she shouted, mashed into a silk six-thousand thread count pillow. "Let me die a miserable virgin eating my dinners alone at Chuck E. Cheese! It's not worth the humiliation!"

But then she looked deep into her future and actually saw herself eating dinner alone at Chuck E. Cheese. Sitting there with a slice of Super Combo pizza, dressed in stripes and plaids. She was having one of her premonitions, and this one set off a hundred clanging fire engine bells in her head. This grim picture would *not* be her future, she decided. No matter how much she loved the Super Combo pizza at Chuck E. Cheese.

She roused herself, shook off her fear, reached for her phone, and called JB. As his phone rang on the other end, she saw her life flicker before her eyes. But because not too much had ever happened to her until she'd come to L.A., what flickered was basically only a replay of the last few months. Just as she was pondering how glamorous and full of possibilities (and a whole new fashion sense) her recent life had become, JB picked up.

"Why, if isn't the wondrous and talented Corliss Meyers calling. How's it shakin', kiddo?"

"Hey, JB," Corliss said a little breathlessly. "It's me, Corliss Meyers."

There was a pause on the other end. "Yessiree, I do believe we've just established that," JB finally said. "Long time, no hear, m'lady. What up?"

"Oh," said Corliss, her heart racing at what she'd set in motion, "nothing's up, you know. Just, um, the usual what upness of up . . ." She was headed toward Babble Central, so she downshifted and put her mouth in neutral.

"Ah," said JB, "what would the world be without the distinctive phraseology of Corliss Meyers? You can turn a sentence inside out like nobody I know."

"Thanks, JB," she said, her mind going blank, "you too!" She was now officially entering the zombie zone. She pinched herself on the arm to make herself snap out of it. "Listen, JB," she said, coming back to herself. "You know we've all been invited to the Emmys, right?"

" 'Course I do! I'm already practicing my red-carpet walk. It might not be as fetching as Heidi Klum's, but I think I'll pass muster. Why do you ask?"

"Well," she said, ignoring his strange Heidi Klum comment (and wondering all over again if he wasn't completely gay), "we're all sitting together and I just thought it would be fun or something if we, you know, sat together."

"Um, didn't you just say we were all sitting together? Or did I miss something?"

"Right, sure, yeah. We are all *sitting* together." She'd backed herself into a wall. She had to think on her feet. In other words, *lie*. "But, um, here's the thing. There was a little goof up at the production office and we're short a couple tickets."

"Social catastrophe!"

"I know, right?"

"And you're calling to tell me I'm off the list?"

"No! Totally not. I was wondering, instead of causing a big stink, if you, we—that is, you and me—shouldn't maybe, I don't know, just go together."

There was another pause on JB's end of the line. This one was longer than the one before. Corliss timed it. "Aha," he eventually said.

"Yeah, like friends or something hanging out—with our other friends. We could even go together, like, in the same car, to make sure there isn't any confusion when we get there. I may even be able to borrow my uncle Ross's Bentley."

"Yeah, I could swing with that," JB said brightly. "We'd have to coordinate our outfits, though. And I refuse to wear purple."

Corliss held the phone away from herself and shook her head. Why was she always drawn to the weirdos? But now that JB had consented she knew she had to drive the deal home—and quickly set some terms. "Great. The ceremony starts at five o'clock. I'll pick you up at four. Deal?"

"Deal!"

"Excellent!" said Corliss, disconnecting the call before there were more negotiations. She exhaled long and hard, then threw herself against her pillows and shrieked with laughter. After a few moments, she flipped over and sighed contentedly— calling JB hadn't been so hard after all. In fact, it was kind of fun. Her eyes fluttered and she began to imagine JB, sitting next to her at the Emmys. Looking cute in that "I didn't mean to look cute" way, and smiling at her without his retainer . . .

# Four

Sure enough, JB was looking cute in a "Who knows how this happened?" kind of way. He was wearing a Dries Van Noten three-button peg-leg suit with a Burberry ascot and somehow managing to pull it off. His hair was parted and slicked, which made him look fashionably geeky—not unintentionally geeky—like he usually did. He smiled at Corliss without his retainer, and although there was a piece of cilantro stuck between his two front teeth (from an hors d'oeuvre he'd eaten at the Roosevelt Hotel pre-party), the piece of gum he stuck in his mouth was bound to catch it momentarily. The whole picture was very close to Corliss's dream. And it didn't hurt that she was looking pretty fierce herself.

The Versace couture dress that Donatella had FedExed Uncle Ross was perfection. Made of clingy pink tulle that stopped just above Corliss's knee, it was cinched by a wide waistband of ribbed magenta. The whole thing said "Sexy Fairy Princess Who Isn't Afraid to Show Her Legs." Completing the entire look was a brilliant, light-refracting diamond bracelet borrowed from Harry Winston, courtesy of Uncle Ross's ex-BF Jeremy.

The moment was almost too much. There Corliss was next to JB, seated in a row with all the other 'Bu stars—as if she was one of them herself. She turned to JB and said the first thing that came into her frazzled-dazzled head. "Wow, isn't this amazing? Especially with you and me here as, I mean, just friends just hanging out and not anything more than that, but, you know . . . together!"

JB grinned and moved his elbow against hers. "Once again, Ms. Meyers, you state the obvious in a way that charms."

"Ha-ha," she laughed weakly, moving her elbow away out of nervousness, then moving it back so forcefully that she knocked JB's arm off the armrest. "Sorry! Um, what I meant to say is that it's great we're here just enjoying the night and our friends and it doesn't even matter that we're not a couple or anything."

At the sound of the word "couple," JB's face went white. Corliss looked for the quickest escape route. She was so mortified she could have crawled into the row ahead of them. But then she would've had to climb over Teri Hatcher's hairpiece— and that looked like a mighty hike. Six ginormous ponytails erupted out of an oversized updo on top of the *Desperate Housewives* star's head.

Corliss was trapped. Her only chance at salvation was to redirect attention away from her temporary-psychosis-induced comment. "How you think Teri Hatcher is keeping that on? My money's on double-sided Velcro."

The color came back into JB's face and he leaned over to Corliss and whispered, "I'm not a betting man anymore, Cor, but if I were I'd say it's more like staple gun."

Corliss laughed so hard, she snorted. JB gave her yet another weird look. She was a total wreck. She felt her forehead break out in splotches. Just her luck, her hive medicine had been recalled earlier in the week because it had given two old ladies in Florida night sweats. She'd have to take a page from Max's book and creatively visualize a smooth forehead if she was going to get through this evening in one piece—and blotch-free.

But it wasn't going to be easy. Months' worth of makeovers were coming apart at the seams in the span of a couple hours. Corliss knew she had to pull it together—and fast.

"Oh, JB," she said, throwing her head back as she tried to sound sophisticated. "You really are too, too much." And then she let her hand drop to JB's thigh.

JB looked at her hand. "Are you looking for a piece of gum? 'Cause it's in my *jacket* pocket, not my pants." He produced a stick of Orbit and smiled obliviously.

## Two Seats Over—4:56 P.M.

Anushka's date, Tyler, suddenly sprang to attention. He'd been passed out against Anushka's shoulder, with a little train of spittle snaking out his mouth. "Wha—is it over?"

Anushka rolled her eyes and wiped the spittle from her shoulder. "It hasn't even begun, model head," she crowed. If Tyler hadn't just landed a big Abercrombie & Fitch spread (where he was photographed naked, from behind, doing a handstand on a bale of hay) Anushka would have tossed him out of the limo on the 405. But his face—and select parts of his body—were everywhere these days, which meant Anushka could squeeze some good PR out of him.

Sure enough, they'd been met with a blinding storm of paparazzi flashes when they arrived on the red carpet. Besides, spittle or no, Tyler was his gorgeous—if not half-conscious—usual self. Wearing a tan Andrew Fezza check suit and his signature Havana Joe slides, the former farm boy was hotter than Palm Springs on the Fourth of July.

Anushka was looking pretty fierce herself, turned out in a metallic gold Alexander Wang wraparound dress with big, chunky Tarina Tarantino bracelets and necklace. She figured she was certainly in the top two percent of hotness in the room. She sat up a little straighter in her seat and, once she realized Tyler had passed out yet again, she glanced over a few seats to where Rocco sat, not with a date, but with his cousin Patrizio.

Anushka had met Patrizio in the lobby right before they were seated. She had to catch her breath the minute she did. He was one of the most gorgeous men she had ever seen: curly black hair cascading over sleepy brown eyes with full garnet lips that were formed in a perpetual pout. He had a big, Roman nose, too, which made Anushka's knees knock. Patrizio somehow managed to look at once boyish and devilish—two traits Anushka appreciated in spades.

Suddenly, he glanced her way. She coyly tilted her head in his direction and he held her gaze. A small smile appeared on his lips. She matched it with the tiniest smile of her own. Electricity flew back and forth between them in big zigzagging patterns. They seemed to be casting a spell on each other. The moment could have lasted forever had it not been broken by the piercing, jackhammerlike noise generated by Tyler's snores.

## A Few Seats Over—4:57 P.M.

Rocco glared at Anushka. She looked away. "You can't be taken in by her, can you?" he whispered in Patrizio's ear.

"Maybe yes, maybe no," Patrizio said in his thick Italian accent. He adjusted his yellow silk collar and slouched insouciantly in his seat.

"Anushka Peters is the worst example of unbridled Hollywood ambition," said Rocco, who was getting hot under his Zegna collar. His cousin—who'd only been in the country for a few hours—was making eyes at Anushka, of all people. Rocco wasn't going to stand for it.

Patrizio shrugged his shoulders and glanced back at Anushka. His eyes gleamed and his lips parted. "Hollywood ambition? This is not my concern. I think she is, like . . . how you say . . . smokin'?"

Rocco took a breath and tried to explain. "Anushka is beautiful, there's no question. But she's also what we call in this country 'ten miles of bad road.'"

"That means you shouldn't ride on her?" said Patrizio with a mischievous grin. "What a pity."

Rocco sighed. He knew Anushka's powers over men were almost impossible to resist. What was it about her? He looked over to where she sat, her posture regal, as if a queen among her subjects. And yet there was something little-girl-lost about her, too. Covering all that was a naughty veneer that made the entire package explosively attractive.

It was maddening; Anushka was everything Rocco had always hated about Hollywood: unprofessional, untrained, unfeeling. Rocco could see his cousin's attraction, but refused to approve of it. With great effort, he decided he'd scan the crowd for someone—anyone—else to look at.

His eyes fell on Tanya. "What about Tanya?" Rocco said to Patrizio. "Isn't she more the type of woman you usually pursue?"

"Maybe yes," said Patrizio. "This Tanya is gorgeous. But she only has eyes for that surfboard."

Rocco looked over at Trent. "I think you mean *surfer*."

"Besides," said Patrizio, glossing over his cousin's correction, "I do not date girls with rosary beads."


## A Few Seats Over—4:59 P.M.

Tanya was praying to God for strength. Trent looked so yummy to her, so completely and totally twelve on a one-to-ten scale of yumminess, that she was worried she'd drag him back to the Roosevelt Hotel, check in under an assumed name, and lose her virginity all over again.

"Trent, um, can you move your knee a little bit?" she said in her baby-girl voice, the voice she could get anything with. Trent obliged, smiling a dopey, love-glazed smile, and moved his knee. The minute his knee disconnected from hers, Tanya felt a cold spot where it had been, an iciness that shot up and down her leg, radiating pain and suffering and loss.

"That better?" he said, still smiling his catatonic love smile. They'd been drowning in a sea of love delirium for a little over a week. Ever since that ride up into the hills, the night Trent offered Tanya his undying love—and a Jamba Juice fiber boost.

"No," Tanya said, in her pouty little-girl voice—the one she could get anything with. "It's not better, Trent. Can you, like, mash your knee against mine again? Please, oh, please?"

Trent nodded, his mouth hanging open, his eyes misting over in an even foggier blanket of lust, and did as he was told. The minute his knee reconnected with Tanya's, she felt a flush of joy explode from the top of her Imitation of Christ dress to the tips of her Jem + Kim shoes. "Jesus!" she yelped.

Everyone from Anushka on down shot her a look. "Sorry," she said, looking apologetic. "Just getting a little prayer in before the show starts."

She closed her eyes and made her lie real. *Jesus*, she silently said to the heavens, *please give me the strength to, like, not be tempted like Eve was in the garden of . . . um . . . wherever that place was. I love Trent—but I also totally love you, Jesus! Even though you, like, wore a robe and bad shoes and weren't as hot as Trent. Trent is, like, totally wearing*

*a hot Tom Ford suit that is totally driving me completely
crazy! I'll never ask you anything again, Jesus, I swear! I just
want to keep my legs crossed and be a good girl until I'm
married—then I can do it all the time! Amen.*

She sighed and sat back in her seat, keeping her eyes
shut to make sure she wasn't tempted by Trent's stick-straight
blond hair, hanging all choppy in front of his sky blue eyes. Or
his deep, golden tan that basted him like butterscotch. Or his
white, glistening teeth, framed by his kissy, scrumptious, ever-
open mouth . . .

"You okay?" he said next to her.

But she wasn't. And she didn't want to answer. She
was fighting a tsunami of desire within—and that tsunami was
heading for the shore! She tried to banish Trent entirely from
her mind, but in an instant he flashed behind her eyelids. First,
dressed as he was sitting next to her, all red-carpet hot. Then he
appeared outfitted in a cape and mask, swooping down on her
like Zorro, with a rose between his teeth and a look of hunger
in his eyes. Then she saw him bare-chested, paddling a canoe
down the Amazon. Finally, Trent appeared as George of the
Jungle, wearing the skimpiest leopard-print thong and yodeling
her name as he swung past her on a big vine . . .

"Mother Mary!" Tanya called out again.

She creaked open her eyes. Once again everyone was
looking at her. "Okay, Tans," said Anushka, "enough with the
praying. This is the Shrine Auditorium, not Our Lady of Hot
Panties!"

## Corliss's Seat—5:02 P.M.

Corliss was in a panic. Not only was JB looking at her like she was the Queen of Looney Land because of her inept pass (which he mistook for a chewing gum grab), but she suddenly couldn't find her Harry Winston bracelet! It was two inches wide, so she was completely mystified as to how it could have left her wrist—let alone be nowhere in sight.

She got on her hands and knees in the aisle and began to search. It wasn't exactly a ladylike position, but what could she do when there was $40,000 of gems at stake?

"Nice view, Ms. Meyers," said JB, speaking to her pink Versace butt.

"Ha-ha-ha!" Corliss laughed way too hard. "It's just my program slipped down here somewhere . . ." She didn't want to tell JB she was about to be arrested for grand larceny. She didn't think that information would bring them any closer to a makeout session.

## The Seat Next to Corliss—5:03 P.M.

JB was worried about Corliss, who was crawling on her hands and knees in the row and smiling at him like a crazy person. In fact, she'd been acting weird ever since she'd rolled up to his place in her uncle's chauffeured Bentley.

"You okay, m'lady?" he ventured, then offered her his hand. He helped her back into her seat and she immediately started cracking her knuckles. She was also blinking a lot.

"Need some eyedrops?"

"No, my eyes are wonderful," she said in the oddly formal voice she'd been using on and off that night. "Never better, in fact. In fact, I'm absolutely a-okay. Whyever do you ask?"

"Um," said JB, not knowing how far to push it, "because you keep saying things like *whyever* and you were just crawling around in the row on your hands and knees in Versace couture. And now you're smiling at me with big, crazy-person eyes."

"I am?" she said, smiling with big, crazy-person eyes.

"'Tis true! You look a little like you just got sprung from the Cedars-Sinai psych wing with a fistful of uppers. Something on your mind?"

"No! Nothing at all!" Corliss exclaimed, her eyes growing even wider and blinking even faster. "Just excited that the show is about to begin," she said, cracking her knuckles again.

"Are you sure?" he said. "I mean, you look like you might be having a seizure. You can tell the Jeebster if something's wrong, ya know. We're old friends at this point, right?"

Corliss bounced up and down in her seat like a toddler who needed to get to the potty. "Of course we are! That's *exactly* what we are—*friends*."

"Boy, you sure are putting a lot of words in italics," JB said.

Corliss threw her head back and laughed way too hard again. "HA-HA-HA! Whatever do you mean, JB?" she said, her eyebrows as wild as deranged caterpillars.

JB was mystified by her odd behavior. "What is it, Corliss? You've got the Jeebster a little worried."

"What is it? I'll tell you!" she whispered into his ear. "The

Harry Winston bracelet that Uncle Ross lent me courtesy of his ex-BF Jeremy is stuck on Teri Hatcher's hairpiece!!!"

Sure enough, $40,000 worth of diamonds were dangling off Teri Hatcher's updo.

"What do I do?" said Corliss helplessly.

JB had no idea. He'd never been in such a situation before. The diamond bracelet swung like a mini-chandelier from the top of Teri Hatcher. "Corliss, how on earth did you manage that?!"

"I have no idea! I think I used way too much moisturizer on my arms and the bracelet must have slid off when I was taking my seat!"

The whole episode was a public relations nightmare. There was no delicate way out of the predicament. Corliss couldn't tap Teri Hatcher on the shoulder and embarrass her with such a revelation. Nor could she yank the bracelet from Teri Hatcher's head without doing some serious fake-hair damage— the bracelet had already taken root.

"Okay," said JB. "I've got a plan. I'll tap Teri Hatcher on the shoulder and distract her with some light conversation. While I'm doing that, you go in and dig out those diamonds. Sound good?"

"Uh-uh," said Corliss, looking completely overwhelmed.

"Oh, Miss Hatcher?" said JB, tapping Teri Hatcher's shoulder. "I just wanted to tell you how much I admire your work!"

Teri Hatcher turned to thank JB—and Corliss gave a quick tug on the bracelet. Miraculously, it came loose—but with one of

Teri Hatcher's ponytails attached.

"Ohmygod!" despaired Corliss, cradling $40,000 worth of diamonds in one hand and hundreds of dollars worth of Hatcher hair in the other. "JB, what do I do with *this*?" She flung the hair in JB's lap as if it were a poisonous spider.

"Well," he said, looking down at the locks, "my first thought was that you could auction it on eBay, but those days are over for me!"

"This is terrible, *mortifying*. You must think I'm a total nut job . . ."

"Well, you do seem a bit strung out tonight, Cor . . ." Corliss's face fell. "Okay, here's what we do. I brought some bobby pins to keep my hair in place until the forming cream set—"

"You did?" asked Corliss incredulously.

"Little trick my sister taught me." JB produced the bobby pins. "Now that Teri Hatcher and I are old friends, I'll engage her once again in some back and forth about how faboo she is."

"You will?" asked Corliss, weakly.

"You'll have to work fast—I'll probably only have her attention for a few seconds, tops." He handed over the bobby pins and the hair extension. "Can you handle this?"

"Uh, I think." Corliss looked like she was about to get seriously sick. She fastened three of the bobby pins to the top of the hair extension, then held it up right behind Teri Hatcher's head. "Okay, I'm ready. I guess . . ."

JB nodded and cleared his throat. "Oh, Ms. Hatcher?" he said, tapping her once again on her beautiful shoulder. Teri

Hatcher turned and smiled again. Corliss immediately went to work. "I forgot to tell you how I think you're the absolute *bestest best* on the show and how I hope it runs forever!" JB said to the star. Teri Hatcher nodded politely and thanked him yet again. She then turned back in her seat. Behind her, Corliss was still trying to get one good bobby pin securely into the updo. Time seemed to slow. JB watched, as Corliss—with a look of sheer panic on her face—poked and jabbed at Teri Hatcher's head. Her hand was shaking so much, JB wondered if it would slip, taking even more ponytails with it. And then . . . *voilà*. Corliss gave one final thrust, and the ponytail was back on Teri's head. It worked! The ponytail seemed a little precarious—and not as artfully placed as it had been—but it was in there, nestled among the rest of the Hatcher hair.

"JB, I'm totally wrung out," said Corliss, panting as she tried to catch her breath. "I don't know how to thank you. That could have been the end of my career! Not to mention the end of our, er, 'hanging out.' But it's not, *is* it?"

"Uh, no, Cor. There's nothing I like more than a friend in emotional freefall on one of Hollywood's biggest nights." He laughed to make her feel better, but he kinda half-meant it. *What's going on with her?* he wondered.

## The Seat Next to Tanya—5:06 P.M.

Trent knew everyone was staring at him and Tanya, but he didn't care. He was in deep—way deep. He got up in the morning and he thought about Tanya. He went to bed at night and thought about Tanya. He picked sand out of his bellybutton and thought about Tanya. He bent over to try and tie his flip-flops and thought about Tanya.

"I, like, think about you, like, all the, like, time," he said for the tenth time that evening. Tanya's face was a mask of delirious happiness. "Sometimes I even, like, think about how much I think about you and then I'm, like, whoa, that's a lot."

"Trent," she said dreamily, "you can't possibly think about me as much as *I* think about me."

But he did. He thought about Tanya so much he was losing the little bit of mind he had. Mostly he was thinking about Tanya taking a bubble bath . . . or Tanya washing his Cruiser with a big, sudsy sponge in slow motion . . . or Tanya opening a gigantic bottle of champagne that sprayed all over her white T-shirt as she giggled and writhed . . .

He was a red-blooded American surfer, for God's sake. Or at least he played one on TV. He had needs. Tanya had to have needs, too. *Why is she holding out on me*, he wondered. Then his mind started to wander . . . maybe she *wasn't* holding out on him. Maybe she was getting her needs met elsewhere . . . Before she was revirginized, she'd had quite a time doing everyone within firing range. Maybe she was up to her old tricks!

Trent's blood boiled as his head filled with adulterous scenarios. He squinted down the row at Rocco. Then he looked two rows over at Justin Chambers. Then turned his head and stared back a couple rows, narrowing his eyes at Raven-Symoné. *With Tanya's past*, Trent thought, *she could be doing any of them.*

Then it hit him like a coral reef. The only way to banish such jealous thoughts from his head and get a piece of some hot Tanya action was to marry her! That way they could do it morning, noon, and night—with Jesus's approval!

Sweat burst from his forehead. He knew he couldn't think too much about it; whenever he thought too much about anything, the space behind his eyeballs hurt. The lights in the theater started going down. The conductor raised his baton, and the orchestra started playing the overture. Trent waited for a minute or two but then he just couldn't hold it in any longer. He just had to kick it out and see what happened. "YOU WANNA MARRY ME OR WHAT?!" he shouted at the top of his voice.

At that precise moment the orchestra took a dramatic ten-second pause.

Every head in the row flicked Trent and Tanya's way as the castmates gasped in unison. Tanya was stone-still at first and then finally muttered an answer—but the music started up again and drowned her out. "What'd you say?" shouted Trent over the horn section.

"I said," Tanya said, shouting back loud enough for her entire row to hear, "can I give you an answer at the commercial break?"

## Pacific Design Center—8:10 P.M.

A cavernous white tent had been stretched between the blue and green ocean-liner-sized buildings of the Design Center. Twirly neon chandeliers hung from rafters, swooping down among the crowd of Emmy-goers as they arrived at the party. An army of waiters in powder blue aprons moved stealthily among the crowd with trays of Wolfgang Puck appetizers: tuna tataki with wasabi whipped cream, smoked salmon with Iranian caviar, black and green tapenade with goat cheese crostini.

Corliss snatched as many as she could and stuffed them in her mouth. "Don't you want any, Max?"

But Max was not hungry. He felt very strange, in fact. Something was wrong; he knew from Corliss's maniacal expression and the way little bits of her hair stood up on end. "What is it, Corliss? You look like gunfire went off somewhere near your head."

"Nothing, Max," she said breathlessly as goat cheese squeezed out through her teeth. "I'm having the time of my life! Seriously." She took a big swallow of tuna tataki and continued. "Well, for a minute there I thought I'd lost this gorgeous $40,000 bracelet." She modeled it for him. "But when I tugged hard on Teri Hatcher it came right off!"

Max had never seen Corliss like this: totally out of her mind and totally gorging on food. It upset him—and he was already upset. At the last minute Michael Rothstein had called him to say he was in bed with the flu and insisted Max take his wife, Mingmei, to the Emmys. This meant Max had to cancel his date with Amy Adams, which had made him *really* cranky.

"Where's Mingmei, Max?" asked Corliss as she licked tapenade off crostini.

"I don't want to discuss it," he said curtly. "I think I've lost her for the time being. She's cornered Oprah and they're having a chat about yo-yo dieting."

Corliss looked over to where Oprah was backed up against a tent pole by Mingmei, who was gesturing wildly. "Hey, doesn't Mingmei have a little thing for you, Max?"

"I said I don't want to discuss it," Max repeated. "I also don't want to discuss the goat cheese schmear on your chin."

Corliss wiped it away with an apologetic look. "Sorry. I worked at a Cracker Barrel in high school and free cheese still makes me go a little nutso."

"TMI, Corliss," said Max, preoccupied with much more pressing matters. "I'd rather discuss who the cast brought as dates tonight. It's very important I know who brought whom."

Corliss looked nervous. "Really? Why?"

"Because I got another memo from Michael Rothstein and the higher-ups at the UBC network this week. Not only do they want to make sure there is no dating among 'Bu staff members, they also want to control the PR spin about who the cast is seen with out on the town. They've invested too much in The 'Bu for our cast members to screw it up by dating *inappropriate* people."

"Ina-a-a-propriate?" Corliss stammered.

"Yes," said Max, staring across the space to one of the bar areas where Anushka was leaning against a table talking to a very hairy young man. "And speaking of, who is that Anushka is with? I thought she was dating that Abercrombie model Tyler . . ."

Corliss looked over. Anushka and Patrizio were wrapped around each other like anchovies in a Caesar salad. "Um, that's

Rocco's cousin. He's visiting from Italy. I think Tyler passed out on top of Jessica Alba . . ." Sure enough, over by the bar, Jessica Alba was struggling to get out from under one stoned A&F model.

"Okay," said Max. "If Anushka's dating Rocco's cousin, I'll need you to dig up all the info you can on him tomorrow morning, first thing."

"But Max," Corliss protested, "they're just talking to each other!"

Max nodded over to Anushka and Patrizio—and raised an eyebrow. The gorgeous couple were now engaged in a serious scrimmage of tonsil hockey. "Talking now, bonking later." Corliss nodded an understanding nod. "Which reminds me, what about Trent and Tanya? We've done a pretty good job keeping them cozy but not too cozy—especially after Tanya admitted on national TV that she's a re-virgin. We have to keep her that way. What's the status there?"

"Well," said Corliss, proceeding slowly, "they mostly seem to be really into each other, Max. But before the lights went down they were talking really loudly about something, so maybe they're having a little lovers' spat?"

"Excellent. We don't want them to get any closer until the second season—which is almost twenty episodes away."

"Well, Max, it's kinda hard to keep two young, red-blooded—"

Max had to cut her off. "And what about JB, Corliss? I heard whispers he actually came with a date! JB, of all people." Max laughed as if this were the most absurd thing he'd ever heard. "Scrawny little, nerdy little JB," he continued. "Can you imagine the kind of girl JB would bring to such an event?" Max chuckled a little more as he imagined the train wreck who might be JB's date.

Corliss turned scarlet.

"What is it, Corliss? Are you having a blood sugar spike after all those appetizers?"

"Uh, no, Max," she said as she twirled her borrowed bracelet and seemed to be stalling. After a bunch of huffing and puffing, she came out with it. "It's just that—that—that—*I* came with JB, Max."

Max reeled and stepped back. Such a coupling had never occurred to him. "You . . . ?" He let it sink in. "I mean, sure, I saw you sitting next to him, but I just assumed you were a seat filler until his real date came back from the ladies' room!"

"No, Max. I was sitting next to him because I was his plus one. Now, don't get upset. It wasn't a *date*-date. At least not to me . . ." She looked a little sad about this. Then she suddenly looked crazy happy. "HA!" She was all over the map emotionally. Was his prized assistant having the kind of breakdown he *himself* usually had? "It was just two friends hanging out with their friends . . ." She teetered off one of her heels. "Oops."

"Aha," said Max, not knowing whether to believe her. She certainly looked guilty about *something*. "That's good to hear, Corliss."

"It is?"

"Yes," he said solemnly. "You'll recall I made a rule that dating among the staff is forbidden. Remember when Petey was bothering you?"

"Oh, yeah . . ." said Corliss, teetering off her other heel. "But—but—as I said—it wasn't a *date*-date. It was so a *not* date-date. So no worries there. Zippo. Nada."

Max shook his head to clear his mind. He decided to take Corliss at her word. The alternative was too odd to contemplate: Corliss and JB getting nasty? He'd keep tracking this odd little romance, but for now he'd pretend he'd never heard about it. He resumed a neutral, nonjudgmental conversational tone. "Where is JB, by the way?"

"Oh, um . . ." Corliss looked around. "He went to the bathroom." She checked her watch. "About an hour ago . . ."

## Somewhere in the Hills of Beverly—3:03 A.M., the Next Morning

Babes of '*Bu*-land!

Get ready for some news that needs some musical accompaniment!

### CUE: NORAH JONES ON SPEED!

That devirginized and revirginized vixen
Tanya Ventura, the lovely Latina we all can't
stop making fun of, the stick-size model from
Manhattan who still has trouble with long
division . . .

## DRUMROLL PLEASE

. . . is betrothed to that yummy blond surfer,
Trent Owen Michaels! As of 2-2-2-night! Ain't
that delish?!?!

Apparently Mr. Michaels popped the question
just before the start of tonight's Emmy Awards
and he had his answer a few excruciating hours
later! Now those two horny children can start
planning a ceremony AND Tanya's
de-revirginization.

Phew! I can feel the heat from here ;)p They
better start making a list and checkin' it twice.
That couple is on *fuego*!

I'll keep you posted as the big day gets closer,

but they're talking SOON and BIG
and CELEB-STUDDED. Looks like the
wedding of the year!

Yours *'Bu*-for-two-ly,
**MBK**

# Five

Corliss woke up in a cold sweat. She'd been dreaming she was a contestant on *Dancing with the Stars*, where she was paired not with a B-level TV star from the mid-nineties but with, of all partners, Legend. He was a terrible partner, stepping on her toes and shouting at her. "If you knew the stepth, I wouldn't be thsteping on your toeth!" Corliss in turn broke down in tears before the judges—and broke out in hives before the TV cameras for all of America to see. She said she had no one but herself to blame for not finding Legend a nanny and the judges scored them the lowest before kicking them off the show.

Thank God someone rescued her from this nightmare by pounding on her door. She hoped it was Uncle Ross's cook bringing her his famous eggs Benedict on blueberry toast. She leaped from her bed, took a quick look in the mirror (her hair was still the same sprouting mess of hairspray and angst from the night before), threw her old, tattered robe around herself, and went to open the door as the knocking continued. "Hold yer horses, I'm coming!"

When she opened the door she found not a plate of yumminess on a silver platter but . . . JB. He stood in the hallway looking down at his Jack Purcells. Corliss pulled her tattered robe more tightly around herself and tried to pat her hair down. "JB . . . ?"

"Hey, Cor," he said, avoiding her eyes.

"What are you doing here? How did you even get IN here? Uncle Ross has a security system that makes the Pentagon seem like a public park!"

"Well, I tried your phone but it went to voice mail. So then I looked for your address on the contact sheet and just came over. Your uncle Ross let me in. In fact, he was encouraging me to use the Jacuzzi if I wanted. Nice guy!"

"But," she said, confused, looking at the clock, "it's not even eight, and we're not called until later today . . . is everything okay?"

"Yeah, things are aces," he said, looking at his sneakers again. "I just wanted to . . . to . . ."

"Is this about last night?" she said, fearing he was there to tell her he never wanted to "hang out" with her again. She wouldn't blame him. She'd behaved like a crazy person in couture. "I'm sorry I acted like a total dork last night. I just got a little nervous—because of the bracelet, of course. Not because you and I were 'hanging out.'"

"Naw, Cor—it was two tons o' fun. I'm just real sorry I went missing there at the end. Not cool!"

"Yeah," said Corliss, still hurt that she had to travel home alone in Uncle Ross's Bentley with the driver asking her where her date had gone. "I was kinda wondering about that . . ."

"Well, see, I went to the restroom and got into this long discussion with Jack Osbourne, who was in the stall next to me. Apparently, he's just as much into *Star Wars* as I am!"

"Wow," said Corliss, not knowing what to say. "That sounds really interesting."

"It was! But next thing I knew, I came out and you were gone. I feel like a Class-A bonehead. Is there any way I can make it up to you?"

Corliss studied JB's expression. He looked sincere enough. In fact, he looked pretty cute this morning in his faded Le Tigre polo and his madras shorts. She quickly asked herself what Uncle Ross would do. *Forgive and forget*, came the answer. And then *Ask him out again*. "Well, I guess we could try, um, hanging out again, maybe? If you wanted? If you had the time?" She tried patting down her hair again.

"Sure!" JB said quickly. "What did you have in mind?"

Emboldened by his fast response, she searched her mind for an innocent-seeming activity they might both enjoy. "You like putt-putt golf?"

"Um, you mean those miniature golf courses that have themes like giants or animals, or giant animals?"

"Yeah. But this one's in Culver City and it has a

glow-in-the-dark theme. You go at night and everything glows! It's pretty cool."

"At night, huh?"

Corliss could tell JB was mulling it over. "Yeah, it's called the Putting Edge. Are you free Friday night?" She couldn't believe how forward she was being.

"The Putting Edge! Well, you know how much I like geeky wordplay. Sure, Cor. Let's do it."

"Great!" she said, overjoyed that she was moving this dating thing forward.

"So you wanna ride to the set?"

"Well, our call isn't until noon because of last night. So if it's all the same to you, I wouldn't mind tucking myself back in bed for a few more Zs."

"Don't you think Max will want to talk to you sooner than noon?"

"Why?"

"Um . . . you haven't read The 'Bu-hoo yet?"

"No, I just woke up. That's why my hair's all rat's-nesty and I'm wearing my bathrobe. Is there anything wrong?"

"Maybe you should have a gander and then decide." JB whipped his iPhone from his shorts and opened to The 'Bu-hoo. As he held the phone up for Corliss to see, her eyes grew wide at what she read . . .

### Tanya's Condo at the Beach—9:32 A.M.

Corliss banged on the door for the fifth time. But there

was so much sound coming from inside no one heard her. "Tanya, open up!"

Eventually the door flew open. Inside was a morass of stylists, florists, and champagne delivery boys climbing all over one another. It looked like West Hollywood on a Saturday night. Sandwiched way in the back, besieged by requests to sign this and accept that, was Tanya in a big, fluffy, terrycloth, thigh-grazing bathrobe. "Corliss!" she called out. "I'm way over here," she said.

Corliss motored over, elbowing her way through the crowd of strangers. When she reached Tanya, she threw her arms around her. "I can't believe it! I read The 'Bu-hoo when I got up this morning and there it was!"

"I know!" squealed Tanya. "I don't know how everyone found out, but it's true, Cor! I'm going to be Mrs. Trent Owen Michaels! Isn't that the bestest best?!"

"It's amazing, Tanya," said Corliss, plucking a fluted glass of champagne out of her friend's hand and moving her into the bedroom so that they could talk.

"What is it?" asked Tanya. "Aren't you happy for me?"

"I'm totally happy for you, Tanya," said Corliss, sitting Tanya down on the bed. "I just want to make sure you've thought this whole marriage thing through."

"What do you mean? I love Trent. We're going to be man and wife. Which means we can do it without burning in hell." The look on Tanya's face was so uncomplicated, so full of simple joy at the solution, that Corliss could only smile.

"Well, that of course—the doing it without burning in

hell business—is *one* of the perks of marriage, Tanya. But what I meant was you're not even twenty years old yet! Marriage is a commitment that lasts a lifetime—or at least a part of a lifetime if you're my mother. I mean, sheesh, it's such a big deal."

"Corliss," said Tanya, patting her hand, "you're way too worried about this. Besides, I know in my heart it's the right decision. The most amazing thing happened to tell me so! Do you want to hear?"

"Of course I do, but—"

"But if I tell you, you can't tell anyone 'cause they'll think I'm more ditzy than they already do!"

"What is it? You can trust me, Tans."

Tanya took her hand, led her into her walk-in closet, and shut the door. Once they were plunked down on the floor in a pile of teeny-weeny bikinis, thongs, and halters, Tanya spoke in a reverent whisper. "Okay, this is going to sound completely nutso—but it's true. The Virgin Mary came to me in a dream."

Corliss cocked her head. She wasn't sure she'd heard right. "You mean Jesus's mother?" Tanya nodded slowly and Corliss immediately worried for her friend's mental health. "Are you sure?"

Tanya's chocolate-colored eyes were the picture of seriousness. "*Totally* she did. It was amazing. First of all, she's really pretty. Like, so much prettier than she is in pictures."

"Um—in pictures?"

"And second of all," continued Tanya breathlessly, "we had this totally amazing conversation where she was like,

'I am the Virgin Mary' and I was like, 'I totally know!' And then she was like, 'You know I'm a virgin, right?' And I was like, 'Yeah—that's why that's your name!' And she was like, 'Totally,' and I was like, 'So what's up, Virgin Mary?' and then she got all, like, scary. With a big scary face. And then she said it. The thing that made me decide to say yes, I'll marry Trent."

The story was ludicrous, but Corliss was enthralled. "What was it? What did the Virgin Mary say?"

"She said, 'Don't end up like me!'" Tanya sat back, as if to let Corliss absorb it. "And then I was like, 'But why not? You're so pretty,' and she was like, 'But I'm a virgin, which totally sucks,' and I was like, 'OHMYGOD, YOU ARE, THAT'S THE WORST!'"

"Tanya, wait, whoa, take it way down. Are you telling me—?"

"I swear, I swear, Corliss. The freakin' Virgin Mary! She said Trent's name and everything. And Trent was asleep on my couch out there, all curled up asleep—groaning in pain like usual whenever he crashes here and I refuse to have sex with him—and I went in and woke him up and said yes!"

"Wow, Tanya, I don't know what to say. . ." She truly didn't. Tanya certainly seemed like she believed what she was telling Corliss. But Corliss was pretty skeptical about a Virgin Mary sighting in the Malibu area.

"You don't *have* to say anything, Corliss. Just say you'll be a bridesmaid!"

Corliss's mouth flew open. Never in her wildest dreams

back in Indiana-no-place did she ever imagine that someone like Tanya—a world-famous *Sports Illustrated* cover girl—would ask her to be a bridesmaid. In spite of the deeply strange nature of the entire conversation up to this point, Corliss was genuinely flattered. "Seriously . . . ?"

"Totally seriously! I'm going to have about twenty bridesmaids so I can afford to make one of them you! Please, oh, please say yes?!"

"Gee, Tanya, when you put it that way . . ."

"I'm going to have a *humongous* wedding with, like, a dozen flower girls and lots of silk draperies all draped over everything in, like, a huge church with all my cousins flying in from all over and a salsa band."

"Wow, you sure are planning quite the event . . ."

Tanya grew serious again. "Would you tell Max?"

"Max! Me? Why not you?"

"Please, oh, please? I'd totally love for him to throw me and Trent a party at his house. It has those amazing views and he lives near so many famous people I want to invite! But I don't want to ask him myself and seem all grabby, ya know? Ohmygod I just had another idea! We could get *Star* magazine to sponsor the party! They could buy the photo rights, too, which should be about two hundred grand."

Corliss was confused all over again. She'd never known Tanya to be so calculating. What could be going through her gorgeous brunette head? "Photo rights . . . ? Where are you getting these—"

"And maybe Wolfgang Puck could cater it! Wouldn't

that be fierce? We'd really get a lot of publicity out of that. And Max *loves* publicity. Please, oh, please ask Max for me?"

Corliss panicked. After her conversation with Max the night before, she was completely certain Max wouldn't take this marriage news well at all. And there was no way she could ask him to throw Tanya and Trent an engagement party. She knew Max and the higher-ups at the UBC had a whole plan about when Trent and Tanya could *date* each other, but she was pretty sure they never factored in marriage. But then again . . . maybe they would be happy about it. A big splashy wedding could be *excellent* for publicity. It all depended on how Corliss spun it for Max . . .

Corliss decided she'd figure it out later. "Sure, Tanya. I'll tell Max—and somehow ask him about a party. Consider it my first wedding gift to you."

Tanya looked confused. "Does that mean you aren't going to buy me an expensive present? I've already registered at Tiffany's."

Before Corliss could answer Tanya's latest whopper, her phone rang. She scrambled for it in her bag and saw that it was—Max. "Hey, Max," Corliss said, answering it. "Were your ears ringing?"

"Why would my ears be ringing, Corliss?" Max replied in his most humorless tone.

"Um, it's a saying? Like when people are talking about you?"

"Corliss, I can't entertain your cryptic form of communication this morning. I need you in my trailer ASAP."

"Righto, Herr Captain. I'm on my way." She hung up and hugged Tanya hard. "I'm really happy for you guys."

Tanya hugged her back. "Thanks, Cor. You're the best! But wait a second," she said, pulling away from Corliss. "Were you on a date with JB at the Emmys last night or what?"

"Me and JB? Ha! That's funny!" Corliss was suddenly shouting. "Naw, we're just friends. F-R-I-E-N-D-S!"

"Cor, I might not be the sharpest knife in the drawer but I certainly know how to spell *friends*." Tanya made her pouty face. "Well, that's too bad. You two would make a pretty cute couple."

"Ya think so? Never crossed my mind," Corliss said, standing up, pulling herself together, and heading out of the closet. She didn't want to engage Tanya—or anyone in the cast— about JB until she knew exactly what was going on between them. "I'll talk to Max, don't you worry. It's totally amazing you and Trent are getting married, Tanya." She suddenly meant it. "Two people like each other not just enough to date—but to spend their entire lives together!" The thought blew Corliss's mind.

## Max's Trailer—9:46 A.M.

"What is it, Max?" said Corliss, who'd jogged all the way from Tanya's condo. "I didn't think you'd be in until later. What with the Emmys and all last night." Corliss wondered if he'd read The 'Bu-hoo yet this morning. She gritted her teeth and hoped he hadn't.

There were deep rings around Max's eyes. "Please don't mention last night, Corliss. I was up until 4 A.M. with Mingmei Rothstein discussing our astrological signs and trying to find excuses why I couldn't give her a full-body massage."

"Yikes."

"And this morning I come into the office to find even more bad news." He opened his jar of painkillers, popped a few, and crunched them.

Corliss winced as Max crunched. "Nothing about any one of our stars, I hope?"

He gave her a desperate look. "Not unless you consider Legend one of them."

Corliss sighed. "Uh, not exactly." She felt terrible that she still hadn't been able to find a nanny for Legend. His presence always seemed to weigh on Max in a way Corliss didn't really understand. Then again, she never had to take care of a hyperactive preschooler with an unhealthy interest in bodily functions. "What is it this time, Max?"

"He egged the camerawoman's Subaru Outback." He pointed out the window of his trailer in the direction of the carnage. Sure enough, there was the camerawoman's Outback, glistening and sticky yellow in the morning sun. "It's embarrassing enough having that kind of car parked next to my Porsche Boxster, but to have it covered in eggs is really too much."

Corliss pretended to be as appalled as Max—"That's terrible!"—even though she found it pretty funny.

"The higher the sun gets in the sky, the more the paint

on my Porsche absorbs the smell. I might have to have the whole thing repainted. And macadamia metallic is hard to duplicate."

"Want me to run a hose out there and take care of things, Max?"

"No, thank you. I've just dispatched twelve of my assistants with toothbrushes. What I *do* need you to do is *please, please* focus on the nanny search. I'm dangerously close to the end of my last good nerve, Corliss, and we've got some very important scenes to shoot this week."

His manicured hands were actually trembling. Corliss knew she had to comfort him—but she didn't want to sugarcoat the truth. "I've been trying, Max, I really have. But it's extremely hard to find a top-notch nanny in a city full of rich people who don't want to take care of their own children. Nannies go like *that*." She snapped her fingers; Max flinched.

"Corliss, no snapping fingers."

"Sorry." She pulled up an Eames stool and gave Max her most compassionate look. "What in God's name are your parents doing on safari for so long anyway?"

Max glanced at his iPhone despondently. "Apparently my father is in the African desert riding on top of some elephant that doesn't get reception."

Corliss thought this was strange, but she certainly wasn't about to argue with Max when he was in a state like this. "Okay, Max, I'll clear my desk and focus on nannies. I've still got a few tricks up my Midwestern sleeve. You know I never let you down." She started for the door, full of resolve.

"Just one nanny, that's all I ask!" he pleaded, rising from behind his desk, his girly upper-register voice rising with him. "It can't be impossible to find one competent child-care worker for one little tyrant! I'm desperate, Corliss," he said, crunching more painkillers. "Legend and his antics have a bigger effect on me than you realize."

Max was totally worked up. He was now chewing the end of his beloved Gucci glasses. "Calm down, Max. You'll work yourself into a tizzy. I'm on it—seriously. In fact, when I got to the set today there was a message from that nanny's agent—the Scientology-approved one I mentioned? She looks excellent on paper. In fact, she survived three months as Britney Spears's nanny."

"That *is* impressive," said Max, suddenly looking hopeful.

"Right? So I called the agent back and he said he'd do his best to determine her interest. Apparently she's in pretty high demand." Corliss hoped this would placate Max for the time being. And she realized now was absolutely *not* the time to tell him about the Trent and Tanya engagement. The news, coupled with the lack-of-nanny hysteria, might send him kerplunking off the deep end.

"Thank you, Corliss. Keep me posted if she or her agent calls."

"Will do, Max." As Corliss turned for the door, her phone rang. She rummaged for it in her bag. The caller ID said MAX'S ASSISTANT #3. She rolled her eyes and answered it. "Yes?" These boneheads of Max's were usually calling with some ridiculous bit of useless information, like, "Max is twelve yards from set, look sharp!" But as she listened she realized *this* time they were calling with some real news. News that seemed heaven-sent.

She turned back to Max to fill him in. "She's here, Max! *That nanny.* Apparently she was on the west side and her agent got through to her so she thought she'd stop by. She's just pulled into the parking lot!"

Max's face opened up like a child's on Christmas morning. "Don't just stand there, Corliss," said Max, rushing to take her by the arms and shake her. "Get out to that parking lot and book that nanny!"

## The Parking Lot—Less Than a Minute Later

Corliss arrived, huffing and puffing. At the edge of the lot, was a convertible, fire-engine red Karmann Ghia, circa 1972. Sitting squeezed into the driver's seat was an extremely pretty middle-aged woman with big, puffy blond hair and an even bigger, puffier pair of bazoombas. "Are you Corliss?" the woman shouted in a thick Russian accent. Corliss nodded, beholding the strange and wonderful vision in front of her. "I'm Olga Rachmoninoff! Best nanny outside Minsk."

Olga vaulted out of the two-seater without opening the door. She was an awesome example of post-forty dexterity. Outfitted in a crisp white Brooks Brothers men's button-down shirt, Capri pants, and espadrilles, Olga strode up to Corliss with a brown leather satchel, took out her résumé, and handed it over with a big, capable smile. "Here is all about me. With the references you can't beat."

"Thank you, Olga. Wow. You came at just the right time! I was about to give up on the nanny search."

Olga leaned in to Corliss and whispered confidently, "You never have to give up with Olga around." Then she winked and elbowed Corliss playfully.

Corliss liked Olga's style. She was fun, but still respectful. Stylish without coming off like a hoochie mama. And so sturdy-looking she seemed like she could take down a redwood without getting a splinter. Maybe Legend had finally met his match. Corliss would have to put the two of them in a room to find out.

"I'm sure your references are stellar, Olga, but I did want you to meet Legend before signing on."

"Of course," said Olga, tilting her chin up confidently. "I meet the little rascal and then we take it from there."

"*Rascal* is the word for him, too—full disclosure!" replied Corliss. "But he's a great kid when you get to know him. He just gets himself involved in some unusual activities. Like today, for instance, he was, um, experimenting with egg yolks."

"Hmm," Olga said thoughtfully, "sounds creative. Let's meet little one."

"Who you calling little one?" snarled someone a few feet below them, caked in egg yolk.

"Legend!" shrieked Corliss. "Aren't you supposed to be in a time-out in Max's trailer?"

Legend turned and shook his plump derriere in Corliss's general direction.

"Legend, don't be so rude—we have a guest." Corliss turned to Olga. "This is Olga Rachmoninoff, the best nanny outside of Minsk."

Olga and Legend stared each other down like two cowboys in a gunfight at high noon.

"You thuppothed to be *my* nanny?"

"You got problem with that?" said Olga sternly, her hands on her hips.

Legend looked Olga up and down. "Naw, I think you're kinda fly." With that, he reached up for Olga's hand, clasped it, and the two of them strolled off down the beach leaving Corliss in a state of amazement.

## A Small Bungalow Farther Down the Beach—A Few Minutes Later

The Bu-Hoo

Holla '*Bu* babes—

It's your pal MBK comin' at you live from da beach. My crack might be sandy but my heart's in the right place!

But it's not MY heart you give a flying flip about, is it? NAH. Not my crack, neither! LMCO (that stands for LAUGH MY CRACK OFF). You wanna hear what all those horny *'Bu* kiddies are up to on America's hottest new TV show, dontcha???

Well hang on to your bikini bottoms 'cause you is in for a treat. We got love, we got romance, we got intrigue!

## BADABING BADABOOM!

First up? That delectable duo Trent and Tanya. Since those two will soon become one, joined together eternally in holy matrimony, we're going to mash them up and call them T&T!

## CUE: DYNAMITE SOUND!

Dat's 'cause it's an explosive combination

(HEHE). Okay, some of you might remember Clueless Meyers calling them that, but that's when she was trying to keep them apart for the sake of *The 'Bu*! Now that there's no way—NADA—of keeping them apart, because they are closerthanthis, I get to steal T&T from Clueless and use it as my own!

Sorry, Clueless!

But the BEST news about the impending nuptials? M2 is fit to be tied! When Herr Director found out about this little unholy alliance (by checking out The 'Bu-hoo of course!) he went BALLISTIC! The screams were heard from San Diego to Santa Cruz!

**LMCO!**

But M2 can't do nuttin' now! Word's already out by yours *'Bu*-ly. HA!

So now Tanya's planning the biggest

wedding since Pam Anderson first got married to Tommy Lee! We're talking MONSTER wedding. A HOT MESS of a wedding. Don't you wanna be a fly on dat wall?????

No worries—you got MBK. And you can be sure I'll bring in all da spooky wedding news. Boowahaa!

And now I must leave you, my kiddies. There's a festive-looking beachy drink with my name on it heading this way. Yummy!

**BUT WAIT!**

**THERE'S MORE!**

One more little tidbit before I dive into this liquid concoction: There's a new nanny in town named Olga. For some reason she thinks she can handle that terrible tyke, Legend. Thinks it won't be a problem at all! Confident lady, right? Excellent nanny, right?

Stellar references, right?

Only time will tell.

All my *'Bust*,
**MBK**

# Six

Bells were once again going off in Corliss's head. Not alarm bells, no. The bells she always heard when something felt perfect, predestined. And those beautiful clanging bells were because of Olga.

"You like me, no?" asked Olga, who was walking at Corliss's side. Corliss did indeed. Olga had spent a good half hour with Legend, and it was clear that with this nanny he'd finally met his match. After that, Corliss interviewed Olga briefly and determined her to be the perfect nanny. Years of experience, impeccable references, and an attitude that could scare Amy Winehouse straight. All in all, Olga was a twenty-first-century Mary Poppins.

"Olga, I can't tell you how much of a relief it is to meet you. To walk down this beach with you!"

"It's nice day, no?"

"It's a *great* day," said Corliss, kicking sand with her foot as they headed to Max's trailer. "Max is going to be so relieved to meet you."

"Max is good name."

Corliss's wonderment continued as she pondered just how solid-gold Olga's résumé was. "You speak six languages! I mean, that won't really come in handy. Legend can barely speak his own language."

"Olga notice. You know what? I cure this boy of lisp."

"Really?" Corliss had never met anyone like Olga before. Everything seemed to come easily to her. She was the picture of proficiency. She'd even spent time working as a sous chef on a submarine!

"Did I bring up psychology degree at University of St. Petersburg?"

Corliss stopped in her tracks and staggered around in the sand. "Olga, if I was the kind of girl who liked girls, I might just propose right now."

"Olga not lesbian. But many my friends are. We go hiking. Does this Legend like outdoors?"

"Well, he's got a lot of allergies so—"

"I cure him of allergies."

Corliss was over the moon. As they continued moving toward Max's trailer, Corliss saw the next couple of weeks stretch out in front of her. Olga would step in and relieve her of her Legend babysitting duties—which would relieve her of some of the *emotional* babysitting she had to do with Max. That would leave more free time to figure out exactly what was going on with JB.

They arrived at the door to Max's trailer. "So," Corliss said. "Here we are."

"Very nice. Katie Holmes trailer not this good."

Corliss smiled. She just knew this would go beautifully. "Now, let me do all the talking." As Corliss raised her knuckles to give her signature three-quick-raps-in-succession knock, a noise emerged from within. It was an unearthly noise—a cat in heat, maybe?—and so high-pitched as to be almost indecipherable. Whatever was making it was sure in a lot of pain.

"THEY CANNOT GET MARRIED WITHOUT MY PERMISSION!"

Corliss's face fell. Max must have read The 'Bu-hoo. Maybe she should have been the one to tell him after all.

"NO ONE GETS MARRIED HERE WITHOUT MY PERMISSION!"

Max was taking the news much harder than Corliss would have predicted. She was just about to take Olga by the hand and lead her away from the ensuing bloodbath when Max appeared, practically tearing off the door to his trailer in an effort to escape.

When Max saw Corliss and Olga standing there, he froze, his face beet red, his choppy four hundred dollar haircut completely pulled this way and that.

"Um, hi, Max. Bad time?"

Max shook his head and let out the teeniest cry. "Nuh-uh."

"Um," continued Corliss, smiling at Olga as if there wasn't a man in emotional freefall standing in front of them, "I do have some good news, Max. This is Olga Rachmoninoff—Legend's new nanny."

Max looked at Olga strangely. And then, bit by bit, the color came back into his face, and he stood up tall and began to smooth his hair out. He went from a stark raving madman to the picture of serenity in about a minute. Once again, Corliss was amazed at the effect Olga had on people.

Max then extended his hand, and in his dreamiest, most low and resonant and not-girly voice—and with what looked to Corliss like a twinkle in his eye—he said, "Charmed to meet you."

## King's Road Café—12:42 P.M., the Next Day

Anushka sat just outside the front door of the café in Hummer blackout shades, dangerously short cutoffs, and an old Johnny Depp T-shirt she'd bought on Melrose. She was twirling an unlit cigarette. She didn't smoke anymore, but she was still addicted to twirling them. It's what she did when she didn't know what else to do. And since she wasn't in any of the scenes they were shooting today, she was trying to keep herself out of trouble. That's why she'd called Corliss to come into town on her lunch break.

Several photographers flew by in their cars, grabbing shots of her with their high-powered lenses while leaning out of their windows on Beverly Boulevard. A few feet away, a waiter pretended he didn't know who she was, but Anushka sensed he was actually the person who'd alerted the paparazzi. She stuck her tongue out at them as they sailed by. Of course, she knew her manager would call her up when the photos appeared and yell at her for not letting them take some flattering pics, but Anushka didn't care. Not today. She was several iced teas down and in a foul mood. She'd been text-messaging Rocco's cousin Patrizio for the last two hours and he hadn't gotten back to her. This never happened. Boys *always* got back to Anushka.

She wanted to stuff her face with a chocolate chip muffin, she was so angry. But she didn't. She crumpled the cigarette and ordered another iced tea refill. When it arrived, she looked at her phone. Corliss was supposed to have been there over a half hour ago. It wasn't like her to be late. Why was the entire world failing her today, she wondered. Just as Anushka was poised on storming off in a huff, Corliss jogged up to the table.

"I'm *so* sorry, Anushka," she said frantically. "Legend has a new nanny and I've been filing the paperwork all morning. Max has got a confidentiality clause like you wouldn't believe! If you work for him you're never allowed to say the word *fake* in his presence or point out how many times he looks at his hair in the course of a day."

"Whatevs," said Anuhska, "I was fine here by myself being pestered by paparazzi—my only friends."

"Listen," said Corliss, "I'm sorry I've been so busy lately and we haven't had a chance to hang out outside of work to do, you know, girl stuff. It's just been one of those nutso periods where work and, um, other things are all mushing together into one great big ball of, um, obligation. Like a cheese ball with too many expectations."

"Whatevs." Anushka shrugged and pretended like she didn't care. "Look, I'm just bummed because I met Rocco's totally hot cousin Patrizio at the Emmys and we exchanged digits, swapped a little spit, whatev—and now he won't get back to me? Me! Anushka Peters!" More paparazzi flew by. Anushka tore off her Hummers and crossed her eyes.

"I'm sorry to hear that, Anushka. I saw you two—and he was really gorgeous." Corliss fanned herself. "What an Italian stallion—phew!"

"Enough about *my* rotten love life. How goes yours? If it isn't *at least* as bad as mine I'm going to be really pissed off. Ha!"

Corliss laughed. "Just as bad—no worries. But I have hopes . . ."

Anushka leaned in. "Tell, tell!"

Corliss bit her lip. "Okay, but this is just between you and me, okay?"

"I swear on Orlando Bloom."

"Wow," said Corliss, impressed. "I know how you feel about him so I guess you're serious. The thing is this: I need girl advice—about love. Uncle Ross comes close, but he's not the real deal."

"I'm all ears, girl. Bring it."

"Okay, so my thing for JB?" Anushka nodded. "Our not-exactly-a-date thing at the Emmys was a total disaster, but even so, I asked him to go putt-putt golfing with me Friday night!"

"Sounds hot," said Anushka, sticking her finger down her throat like she was making herself retch.

"Anyway, I don't know if it's a date-date or a friend-hang." Corliss lifted and lowered her hands like a scale measuring the possibilities of each scenario. "Date-date" she sent the scales up and "friend-hang" she sent the scales down. "And frankly all this mystery is making me a little impatient. What's a girl from Indiana-no-place to do?"

Anushka sat back in her chair and tapped one perfect fingernail on her perfect chin. "Hmmm . . ." she mused. "Here's what I think, Cor. And I want you to listen closely." Anushka knew she had to be succinct with Corliss, whom she judged to be about middle-school level when it came to dating. "It's very simple: You have to pounce."

"Pounce?!" Corliss shouted. "I can't pounce, Anushka! It's Corliss Meyers you're talking to here. I never left the house until a few months ago! I didn't even go to my prom—I watched it on Web simulcast from under my covers! I couldn't possibly pounce. Sheesh!"

"Cor, listen to me. These boys don't know *what* they want. And we gotta tell 'em. Ya hear? We give them all this power, pretend they should be the ones to make the moves, but take it from Anushka. After the first date if there ain't nuttin' going on, I *make sure* something's going on. Or I'm outta there."

"But how? When? And what do I wear!" Corliss was drenched in sweat.

"Calm down, hot pants. The prescription for pouncing can be found in three words: naked, champagne, hot tub."

"Um," said a terrified Corliss, "that's four words."

"Whatevs. Get him drunk, get him dunked, and get the deed done."

Corliss shivered. "Uncle Ross has a hot tub at the

house, but . . ." Anushka thought she heard Corliss's teeth rattling. " . . . but I don't know if I can do that . . ."

"Suit yourself, Cor. But let me ask you this: Do you want a year's worth of Friday nights spent at putt-putt golf?" Corliss shook her head no. "Okay, then. Do as Mama Anushka says. And tell that waiter dude you want that muffin to go. I've got an appointment at Pat's Tats to get a little star inked behind my ear. I've scheduled an appointment for you, too—as a gift."

Corliss's eyes widened. "Are you serious?"

"Totally. I even came up with a design for you, too. It's real small, and real classy: a little arrow pointing to your cleavage and with the words THIS WAY TO LOVE."

"WHAT?!"

"Kidding," winked Anushka, pushing her boobs together as more paparazzi sailed by, cameras a-blazin'.

### The Ivy on Robertson—9:36 P.M.—That Evening

"But what does it matter?" pleaded Trent as he speared a fistful of rigatoni slathered in tomato sauce and dripping with squid. "We're getting married anyway, right? One night with me slobbering over your hot, naked body can't be that sinful, Tans . . ."

But lately Tanya wasn't so sure she *wanted* him slobbering over her hot, naked body. Ever since she'd accepted his proposal, he seemed to grow up before her eyes, less and less like a sun-kissed beach boy and more and more like . . . her father. Kind of thick in the middle and jowly. "You sure you should be eating carbs this late?" she asked, crinkling her face, more than a little worried about his waistline. "I mean, we did get the tux measurements and it would be so not hot if you came down the aisle all, like, porkin'. Maybe we should call Jenny Crai—"

Trent slammed down the forkful of rigatoni. "Jeez, Tans, avoid my question why dontcha? And no, we are not calling Jenny! I got ribbed enough for being on that housewife diet. Now I just eat sensibly and make sure my glycemic load is, like, low." He looked really miffed.

"Sorry," Tanya pouted, moving some hair from his eyes in a tender gesture, knowing how big his ego could sometimes be. She never forgot that he was once a total player, breaking hearts up and down the coast. That he'd chosen her above all others still seemed miraculous to her. And miracles came from Jesus.

"Look, Trent, we've set the wedding date—and it's only a month away. I know it's hard to wait for this . . ." She opened her arms wide to show him her taut, sinuous body, which at the moment was showcased in a clingy Onna Ehrlich top that hugged her like wet paint. "But just think of how good it will be when you finally get to do me up and down!"

Trent's eyes pulsed with desire. He needed to quell his passion by putting something in his mouth—something with a low carb content. He signaled the waiter, who arrived at their table in a flash.

"Yes, Mr. Michaels, is there a problem?" the waiter said, all butt-kissy and ready to jump into action. "I notice you haven't touched your rigatoni di calamari."

Trent took three quick breaths to calm himself down—and then adjusted his pants. "Uh, yeah, can you bring me the escargot appetizer and a glass of water and give this rigatoni to someone who, like, doesn't care if they're a porker? Maybe that dude over there?" said Trent, pointing in the direction of Tom Cruise.

"Escargot, eh?" the waiter asked knowingly, looking back and forth between Trent and Tanya. "Escargot are an aphrodisiac." He gave the couple a sly wink.

"Is an aphrodisiac something that makes your hair all afro-y?" asked Tanya. "'Cause I just had mine straightened," she said to Trent, "and I thought we were sharing."

"Um," said the waiter, looking dismayed, "an aphrodisiac is a food or beverage that stimulates the sex drive."

"No!" shouted Trent. "I don't need anything that does that, for cryin' out loud! Bring me a PB&J!"

"Trent!" yelped Tanya. "That's all fat and sugar!"

"I'm sorry, Mr. Michaels," said the waiter, looking suddenly very judgmental. "Our kitchen doesn't do grade-school cuisine."

"Then whatever you got back there! No food that will get me horny!" The waiter was mystified. Tanya saw they were causing a scene.

"Trent," Tanya said, leaning across the table to whisper, "you're obviously feeling the strain of my vow of celibacy. I think we need a prayer circle." She took his hand. Then she took the waiter's hand. "Now you take Trent's hand." The waiter did as he was told.

"Tans, why is this dude holding my hand?!"

"A prayer circle needs at least three people, Trent. Now lower your eyes and pray!"

"I don't wanna pray, Tanya. And to tell you the truth, the way you've been acting, I'm not so sure about this wedding business anymore!"

Tanya's jaw hit the ground. Sure, she'd been having her own doubts, but never once would she have considered postponing the wedding.

The waiter tried to move to another table, but Tanya wouldn't let go of him. "Trent, how can you say that? It's way too late for you to be having cold feet. I already got free sponsorship for our entire wedding from Virgin America!"

"Ha!" the waiter snorted. "Sorry," he said immediately. "Um, can we pray now? I've got to serve Salma Hayek at table seven."

Tanya nodded and looked up to heaven as she spoke. "Jesus, thank you for allowing us to have a prayer circle at the Ivy—which I just know would be one of your favorite restaurants if you weren't in heaven because you died for my sins. Make Trent strong until the day we get married—which is gonna happen!" She raised her voice for this last bit. "He loves me, Lord, but he's a total horndog. Amen."

"Amen!" said the waiter, winking at Trent. He then scurried off to get Trent something lean and low-carb.

"Ohmygod," said Tanya, peering into her salad. "Trent . . . do you see what I see in my salad?"

"Um . . . croutons?"

"No! Look at this leaf . . ." She plucked a baby spinach leaf from the bowl and passed it across the table so Trent could see what she saw. "All the little bumps on it form a face. And that face is the baby Jesus!"

Trent pondered the spinach leaf a moment, then turned white as a ghost. His mouth, which usually hung open, was down by his collar. His eyes quivered as if thousands of volts of electricity were coursing through him. "What's the baby Jesus doing in your salad, Tans?!"

"He's, like, looking up at me! And he looks so cute!"

"Tans, I'm really spooked. You know what this means?" She shook her head. "It means, like, you have a direct line to, like, God!"

"Wow . . . like, I've got God's private number or something?"

Trent nodded fearfully. His hay-colored hair grew damp with sweat. He pulled at his shirt as if he were jumping out of his skin. "I swear, Tans, I won't bother you about sex till we're married! I swear on this baby spinach salad where the baby Jesus is! Now let's get out of here. I'm not hungry anymore!" As he took her hand and they fled the Ivy, they were met at the curb by a dozen paparazzi, blinding them with flashes.

"Trent! Tanya!" they called. "Give us a smile! What's wrong? Why the rush?" The valets had Trent's Cruiser waiting, and he and Tanya were able to make a quick escape, tearing down Robertson. As they fled the scene, Tanya looked up to heaven and mouthed a silent thank-you to God.

# Seven

## The Putting Edge—7:24 P.M., the Next Evening

Corliss couldn't pounce. Not in the middle of a glow-in-the-dark golf course, anyway. First of all, she and JB were surrounded by twenty cranky nine-year-olds who were waiting impatiently to tee off. Not exactly the setting for pouncing. Corliss had considered inviting JB over to Uncle Ross's and somehow muscling him into the hot tub—per Anushka's naughty suggestion—but naked hot-tubbing just wasn't her style. No, no matter what Anushka "The Teen Queen of Seduction" said, Corliss knew she'd have to proceed at her own pace.

"If you tap the ball real gently on the far side, JB, it'll knock it in the right direction," Corliss offered helpfully. But then she worried her suggestion might injure his masculine pride. She'd read in *CosmoGirl* that boys didn't really want advice from their dates. She backtracked fast. "Least, that's what little old me thinks! Take or leave! Do or don't! It's your game!" she blathered, unable to stop the torrent of inanities that spewed forth. Finally, she clamped her hand over her mouth.

JB didn't seem to notice. He was still contemplating his putt, oblivious to the groaning nine-year-olds who were giving him and Corliss dirty looks. "You know who's a really good golfer?" said JB, stalling the tee again. "Rocs! He's also good at sailing, apparently. And woodcarving, ballroom dancing, and Legos. He's a pretty good pastry chef, too—have you ever tried his buttery biscuits?" JB licked his lips.

Corliss gritted her teeth. "Uh, no, can't say I have tried Rocco's, um, buttery biscuits," she said, hoping JB would hear just how gay his question had sounded. He hadn't stopped talking about Rocco all evening. It was getting a little weird. In spite of all his protests it was still hard not to wonder whether he was gay. Maybe he was, but he just didn't know it yet? She was going to keep careful track of how many more Rocco mentions the night would hold.

"Those bis-quits are wunderbar!" JB kissed his fingers and threw them into the air. The nine-year-olds behind him shook their heads.

That did it. Corliss couldn't hold back anymore. "You and Rocco sure spend a lot of time together. Are you completely sure there's nothing gay going on?"

JB was taken aback for a moment, then broke out in a reassuring smile. "Cor, m'lady, I swear on a stack of *CosmoGirls*," he said, placing his hand over his heart. "Don't you just love that rag?"

Corliss put her hand on her hip and titled her head skeptically. What straight boy reads *CosmoGirl*? "See, that's another thing," she said patiently. "You gave me that makeover once and you're always offering little tips on how I should wear my hair, or what shoes to wear. That stuff is all really gay, JB."

"What can I say?" JB said, shrugging and still not teeing off. "My meterosexuality is known from sea to shining sea." He squinted again at the ball, which was only three inches from the hole it was meant to go in.

"Just putt already," said one of the nine-year-olds waiting in line behind them. JB looked up at the kid like he'd momentarily forgotten where he was, then swung his club and tapped the glow-in-the-dark ball exactly on the spot where Corliss suggested. It rolled cleanly across the AstroTurf and dropped expertly into the hole.

"You did it!" Corliss said, jumping up and down.

"I totally did!" JB looked like he couldn't have been more surprised. "Thanks to your advice," he said, nudging her elbow.

Suddenly Corliss felt a wave of encouragement wash over her. JB had never elbow-nudged her before. Was it possible that he was flirting with her? "Now we just need to add up our scores," she said with an undercurrent of "I'm flirting right back." Then she took their scorecard over to a park bench and patted the seat next to her. When JB sat, Corliss moved a little closer to him. But then he inched away. So she moved closer to him again. But then he inched away again. This went on until JB inched his way off the end of the bench.

"Sorry," he said, leaping up, red-faced, "my bad! The Jeebster isn't the picture of grace, is he?"

Corliss felt like a total dork. It was like JB was avoiding intimacy at all costs. Maybe her premonitions were wrong for the first time. Maybe she and JB were meant to be just friends. But what about the elbow nudge? And hadn't he said yes when she'd asked him to "hang out" again? And hadn't she just detected on him the distinct smell of cologne—when she'd only ever smelled Mennen Speed Stick deodorant on him before? Was all this the behavior of someone not interested? *Maybe,* she thought. *Maybe not!* JB was sending her so many mixed signals her head felt like sautéed onions.

*Okay,* she thought, *I don't want to live in the dark anymore.* She knew she absolutely had to *somehow* move things forward. Really hit the romance nail on the head—and make no bones about it. "Hey, JB. I have an idea. Why don't we drive up to Topanga Canyon? It's a full moon tonight, and isn't that romantic?"

JB gulped. "Dontcha wanna add up our scores?"

"I already did," Corliss said. "You won. Which means," she said, pulling him down next to her on the bench, "whatever we do next is what *you* want to do next." She waited for him to take the lead, be the man—something she had also learned from the *CosmoGirl* article.

"Well, I am kinda tired, to tell you the truth, Cor. And tomorrow is a pretty big day for me on the set. Would you mind if we just called it a night?"

"No," she said, utterly deflated.

"And then, you know, do something else sometime soon?"

"Yes!" she cried, utterly overjoyed.

As they headed to the cashier to return their golf clubs, Corliss decided that if she wanted to get to the bottom of her relationship with JB, it was time to push herself to the wall. In other words, it was the hot-tub scenario or bust. Even if the thought of trying such a maneuver made her eyes cross. In fact, it occurred to her that securing a little backup to keep from caving at the last minute probably wasn't a bad idea. And who better to back her up than Uncle Ross, who was already overly invested in her dating life (and just so happened to have a hot tub in his very own home)?

"Um, what are you doing later this week, JB? Wanna have dinner at my Uncle Ross's place some night?"

"Free food cooked by other people? Are you kidding? I'm there like a bear at the fair!"

*Not the most romantic response*, thought Corliss, *but it's progress.*


## *The 'Bu* Soundstage on the UBC Lot—10:52 A.M., the Next Morning

The set for this week's episode of *The 'Bu* was a re-creation of the stunning estate in Malibu. The two-story-high blue stone fireplace, the vaulted Tibetan ceiling, the soaring leaded glass windows, the Belgian tapestries, the Murano glass chandelier that dripped thousands of glittering red shards from above—all of it was copied and built in the middle of the vast soundstage.

It was an uncanny replication, perfect to the last detail.

Corliss, who was dressed in some of her cutest gear—a Max Azria cardigan over a Nanette Lepore skirt—whistled long as she took it all in. "Boy, look what a TV show budget will get ya."

"Pretty impressive, I know," said Max at her side. "The network is not sparing any expense with our show—which is a sign they continue to believe in it. I've got to keep them believing in it, Corliss."

"You always find a way, Max." She knew it was good to start the day with a little subtle brownnosing, just to get things off on the right foot.

"Thank you, Corliss," said Max, looking pleased. "And how's the cast doing this morning? Any concerns I should have?" he said, taking in his perfect hair in one of the set's gilded mirrors.

Corliss craned her neck to the far corner of the soundstage, where the makeup technicians were fretting over the cast. She gave JB a little wave with her fingers. He gave her a little wave back. *Good sign,* she thought. Everyone else looked ready, willing, and able—until she spotted Anushka. Anushka was wearing a bikini so small it looked like three tortellinis tied together with tinsel. She was also wearing her bald cap—and sulking. "Um, let me get back to you on the cast concerns, Max," Corliss said in her cheeriest voice, before making a beeline to Anushka. "What is it, Anushka?" she said under her breath. "You've got your crabby face on and you're not even near nap time."

"First of all, Cor, I still can't get Patrizio to return any of my text messages and it's making me crazazy!"

"Anushka, please. We're at work. I'm sorry about the lack of Italian stallion-ness in your life, but it will have to wait till we're on break, okay?"

"Okay, Miss Company Policy," said Anushka, rolling her eyes. "In that case I would appreciate it if you told Max I'd like to play this scene in a gold brocade head scarf with large gold hoop earrings."

"What?! We're prepping the first shot, Anushka. You know how slow the costume department moves."

Anushka just shrugged. Corliss bit her tongue to keep from screaming. But she was becoming smarter. Instead of relaying Anushka's dissatisfaction to Max—which is exactly what Anushka expected her to do—she would defray any potential tension by, well, *lying*. Just a little. "Everyone's in the *greatest* mood, Max," shouted Corliss as she made her way back to her fearful leader. "Really upbeat and ready to work."

"Excellent. I did notice a cheerful energy on the soundstage when I walked in."

"There *is* the tiniest request," she continued, very smoothly, "really very small—from Anushka."

Max hardly batted an eye. "Yes, quickly. Out with it."

"It's really hardly anything at all," Corliss replied, consulting her clipboard to make it look official. And then she told Max about Anushka's request. As she waited for his response, she held her breath and pretended to look through her notes.

For a moment, Max's face was frozen, unreadable. "Fine by me," he finally said. "Alert the costume department." Corliss immediately text-messaged the costume department about the change. "Anything else?"

"Um," Corliss said, silently amazed that she managed to pull that off, "just that the camerawoman has an appointment with her podiatrist at noon so we'll have to break for an hour then."

"Fine as well," Max said, further unruffled. "And Legend? I haven't heard a peep today."

"That lack of peep you hear is good news, Max. Olga has Legend on a field trip to the La Brea Tar Pits. He's learning about the period when saber-toothed cats and mammoths roamed the Los Angeles Basin."

"That woman is a gift from God," Max said, lifting his eyes up to the heavens. "I mean," he said, lowering his eyes, "from L. Ron Hubbard, founder of Scientology."

Corliss coughed to keep from giggling. "No matter who Olga's a gift from, she's in pretty good shape for a woman her age, dontcha think?" Corliss became dreamy imagining herself one day as vigorous—and as shapely—as Olga.

"That's something I'd prefer not to discuss with you, Corliss," he said.

"Those legs . . ." Corliss rhapsodized, not hearing Max. "Those biceps . . . and all that big, blond hair . . ."

"Corliss, your Olga crush is showing again." Corliss snapped herself out of it, going a little red in the process. "Now if you'll excuse me, I need to concentrate." He held his hands up in front of his face, imagining the scene he was about to shoot. Corliss knew this meant he was getting into *his zone* and she started shushing the technicians and actors who were in close proximity. "One thing I forgot, Corliss," he whispered to her, out of earshot of anyone else.

"What is it, Max?" she said, poised to write it down.

His voice became an almost inaudible hiss. "This Trent and Tanya marriage business. I need you to put an end to it." He then raised his hands in the air again, going back to *his zone*, as if he'd just said nothing more controversial than "Bring me my loofah sponge."

"What—what do you mean, Max?" stammered Corliss.

"Corliss, you know exactly what I mean," Max whispered fiercely. "The network is trying to control the PR spin when it comes to the cast's personal lives. There's no way to spin a marriage between a seventeen-year-old and an eighteen-year-old. Only trailer trash gets married before their twentieth birthdays."

Corliss was dumbstruck. She envisioned herself once again as some kind of hiding-behind-plants secret agent, skulking around in parked cars and trying to get cheap, tawdry information out of people whose cheap, tawdry business she wanted nothing to do with. And she knew it was hopeless, anyway: Trent and Tanya were *way* beyond dating. They were getting hitched—no ifs, ands, or buts. And once they were hitched, they were immediately going to *do it*. They had actually planned the date and hour and place Tanya would become de-revirginized. The event involved a thousand rose petals and a J. Lo soundtrack, but that's as much as Corliss could bear hearing about.

"But they're *getting married*, Max," she said, finally betraying her exasperation. "That's an eensy bit more serious than dating, dontcha think?"

"Please, Corliss, look at them." He nodded over to a corner of the soundstage, where Tanya bounced up and down on Trent's lap, elated as a second-grader at Wet 'n Wild. "Do you think those two could be serious about anything?"

"Um," said Corliss, contemplating the really gross spectacle, "point taken, but—but the network really has no business interfering when two people are actually getting married!" she blurted.

"Corliss," Max said, putting his hand on her shoulder, "the network is okay about them *getting married*. If they spin it right, the American TV-watching public would find it romantic. But one thing the network is not fine about is them *getting a divorce*."

Corliss stepped back. Her mouth fell open wide. The thought had never occurred to her. Tanya was a good Catholic girl, for one thing. And Trent, well, Trent was and always would be simply too whipped to contemplate a divorce. "Max, that's so—so—cynical of you. I think they really love each other."

Max didn't look persuaded. "I give them two weeks before one of them files papers—and *that* is something the network does not want to see happen. Or me, for that matter. Can you imagine what it would be like for me to direct *divorced people*? I can barely get my parents in the same room on my birthday." Max moved away from Corliss, raising his hands in the air again, trying to get back into *his zone*.

None of this had occurred to Corliss. And now it was too late. There was no stopping the high-speed train that was Tanya and Trent's wedding. In fact, it had already left the station.

She then approached Max cautiously. She'd been hearing so much about the wedding plans in the last few days and she knew she had to be straight with Max. "I know you're already in *your zone* and all, and there's only a couple minutes until we begin filming, but there's something important you should know." Max rolled his fingers for her to proceed quickly. "Right." Corliss took a big breath of air and spat it out without stopping: "Okay the thing is not only are Trent and Tanya getting married no matter what *you* or *anyone* says, they already got the license *and* they are appearing on *Ellen* tomorrow afternoon to announce the wedding date *and* they've sold the photo rights to *People* magazine *and* they really hope they can convince you to allow them to get married on this very soundstage by converting it into a tropical Puerto-Rican-themed paradise! They also want you to host an engagement party at your house, nothing too big, maybe a few hundred people, sponsored by another magazine, of course, which I think would be a nice gesture." She held her breath waiting for his response.

Max didn't say anything for a full moment. Corliss was beginning to get dizzy the longer he withheld comment. "They're going to be on *Ellen* tomorrow?" he said finally.

"Uh-huh," said Corliss, still not knowing if he'd heard the full story.

"Well, that's very interesting," he replied in a clipped voice. "I had drinks with Ellen last night at the Chateau and she didn't say a thing." He looked hurt. "And I thought I was very close to Ellen. I once took her girlfriend Portia to the Beverly Center to buy a jogging bra. Gestures like that aren't small." He tilted his head up. "Well, I guess you never know who your friends are in *this* town." He looked at his perfect cuticles as if he would cry.

"Um, Max, did you hear what I said? About Trent and Tanya? Getting married and wanting to have the wedding here? Big tropical splash? Hello?"

Max sighed. "Yes, I heard, Corliss. I guess there's nothing we can do if they have a license and they're going to tell the world tomorrow afternoon on daytime television. The only thing we *can* do is spin it for all the press it's worth—and hope the marriage sticks."

Corliss exhaled. "I think that's wise, Max. Besides, how can anyone come between two people so obviously in love?" She looked over to where Trent and Tanya were now giggling and wrestling on the floor.

Max shook his head. "My definition of love doesn't involve nearly so much horseplay." He watched as Trent flipped and pinned Tanya. "Now please make sure Anushka, Rocco, and our two lovebirds are in their places, Corliss. I'm ready to shoot their scene."

"Righto, Max," said Corliss, who then saluted and motored off.

# ★ The 'Bu

## Episode III

INT. A GRAND MALIBU VILLA—DAY

ALECIA, wearing a gold brocade head
scarf with large gold hoop earrings and
a metallic gold string bikini, lounges
seductively on a Moroccan chaise.

RAMONE, his inky black hair windswept, his
dark eyes glowering, enters through the
heavy damask curtains and moves to the
window. The tension between these two is
palpable.

> RAMONE
>
> I thought you'd turned a corner
> after your scrape with death.
> But from what I hear through
> the grapevine, nothing has
> changed . . .

> ALECIA
>
> You're just upset you're still
> attracted to me. But Travis
> loves me now. Even without my
> hair.

                    RAMONE
     That's because—because—(he can't
     help himself) even shorn of
     your beautiful locks, you still
     manage to captivate!


                    ALECIA
     (not taking the bait) Where I'm
     going looks don't matter . . .


STORM CLOUDS roll in off the coast. Rocco's
eyes darken as he shakes his head and
mutters a bitter chuckle.


                    RAMONE
     I see someone's in a dramatic
     mood.


                    ALECIA
     You've never once taken me
     seriously, have you? None of
     my friends have. You all think
     I'm a self-absorbed narcissist.
     Well, maybe you'll take me
     seriously once all of you hear
     what I've put in motion . . .

She lifts herself up with great effort and moves to Ramone's side. They both stare out at the STORM moving in. Alecia's face fixes with resolve.

                    ALECIA
          I've decided to liquidate my
          parents' estate—the houses,
          the cars, the yachts—all of it.


                    RAMONE
          You're not serious.


                    ALECIA
          (She nods.) I'm going to give
          every bit of money I have to
          Greenworld, to save the ozone.
          Once that's done I'm going to
          move to India and become a
          Buddhist nun. I'll subsist on
          rice and handouts. And maybe—just
          maybe—I'll get to know who I
          really am—for once!


Ramone gives a short laugh and moves toward the door.

                    RAMONE
          Send me a postcard.


                    ALECIA
          You don't believe anything I say,
          do you?


                    RAMONE
          What I believe is that you faked
          your own death to get the pity
          of your friends. And now you're
          using your parents' death as a
          means to escape. There's only so
          far you can run, Alecia, before
          you do actually find yourself.
          And when you do, I have a feeling
          it's not going to be very pretty.


As he turns to go, she hurls an ETRUSCAN VASE
at his head, missing it by inches. It crashes
into a GILDED MIRROR on the wall. The mirror
SHATTERS and shards crash to the floor.
Ramone grins.


                    RAMONE
          Seven more years bad luck,
          Alecia. Are you sure you can
          afford that?

And he's gone. Alecia throws herself on the
chaise, weeping. TESSA rushes in, wearing a
hooded terrycloth bathrobe.

                    TESSA
          What happened! I was in the spa
          and I heard a crash! Are you
          okay?

Alecia straightens up and brushes a tear from
her eye, hiding her mortification.

                    ALECIA
          Don't worry about me, Tess. I'm
          fine. I'm just fine . . .

FADE OUT

## The 'Bu Soundstage—12:13 P.M.

"I'm so sorry, Max!" said Tanya with a big frown from under her hooded terrycloth robe. "I totally heard the vase crash into the mirror, which I know was totally my cue, but then I got a call from Jasmine who's doing the catering for my wedding. And she's all like, 'Do you want ganache in the cake?' and I'm all like, 'What's *ganache*?'" Tanya crumpled up her face like *ganache* was the craziest word she'd ever heard.

Trent smiled his crooked grin at her. "Isn't she, like, fierce?"

Anushka and Rocco stood by, glaring at the love-mad couple. The camerawoman kept tapping her watch, trying to remind Max about her podiatrist appointment. And Corliss was just off-set, giggling at everything that came out of JB's mouth.

The inside of Max's head was not a good place to be at this moment. It was a dark, small space where strange, discordant music played on badly tuned violins. "Um, Tanya," he said with all the pretend patience he could muster. "Why don't we try it again, but this time—"

"One sec!" Tanya shouted, putting a finger in the air and answering her phone for the umpteenth time in the last two hours. "Hello?" She covered her phone and announced to everyone: "Ohmygod, it's Marishka, the florist, and she is, like, so totally impossible to get a hold of! And I want lilies, and she's saying orchids, and I'm like, no way!" Tanya took the call, jabbering off into a corner of the set.

The camerawoman stepped forward. "I really have to go, Max. My arches fell yesterday, and I have to be fitted for corrective shoes."

"Just a few more minutes?" Max pleaded.

"You'll recall I have to take the bus because my car's still in the shop getting the egg yolk taken off. If I don't make the twelve-twenty bus I could be on arch support for the rest of my life."

"But we've only done three takes . . ." Max protested.

"Not my problemo," said the camerawoman, lumbering away from her camera and heading off the set. "Call my union." Just then Corliss threw her head back at something JB said and laughed/snorted so loudly that it echoed throughout the soundstage. Max winced and felt a crick in his neck.

"Max," said Rocco, gesturing to where Corliss and JB stood giggling with each other, "the level of seriousness on the set has reached the proverbial low. Is there nothing that can be done to keep 'professionalism' the byword of the day?"

"Whatever, SAT boy," said Anushka wearily. "I'm standing here bald as a cue ball, just waiting for you to say *action*. It's Bridezilla and America's Next Top Husband over here who are gumming up the works."

Trent grinned his crooked, love-drowned grin. "She just wants things to be, like, perfect."

Max massaged his temples with his thumb and forefingers and made a mental note to call the Scientology Celebrity Centre to see if they could get him another counselor.

"For your information," said Rocco to Anushka, "it's not Trent and Tanya who are permeating the air with non-professional behavior."

"What's that supposed to mean?" said Anushka, the color rising in her face. "I'm the picture of professionalism! Here on time, knowing my lines—acting with *wooden* actors who'd rather be, I don't know, maybe *directing*?"

Rocco seethed. "That's no business of yours, Anushka."

"And who your cousin text-messages is no business of *yours*, Rocco!" exploded Anushka, her big hoop earrings jangling. "I know you turned Patrizio against me! You've always had it out for me. And what did I ever do to you, you overeducated muscle boy?" Anushka tore off her bald cap, threw it at Rocco's feet, and stormed off.

"Anushka!" Max was about to head after her when he heard Corliss laugh/snort again from somewhere off-set. His head snapped in the direction of the sound and he got another crick. "Corliss!" he shouted, way up in his girly register.

"Yes, Max?!" Corliss said, appearing instantly. "Is everything okay?"

"No, Corliss. Everything is not okay. I've got one star talking cake, another talking nonsense, another tossing her bald cap, another speaking in a vocabulary that's way beyond my comprehension, and a camerawoman on a bus to her podiatrist." Max counted to ten in his head (but in Spanish, as he was trying to get a date with Jessica Alba). It seemed to calm him down. But then something else occurred to him.

Something that very much did *not* calm him down. "And what are you and JB giggling about? Whenever I need you lately you're off in some dark corner, tossing your head back and laughing way too loudly at something JB is saying."

Corliss blushed deeply. Max looked at Rocco and Trent. They looked away. JB rushed in with that big, open, how-did-I-get-here face he sometimes had. "Heard m'name! Is my order up? Remember, I wanted fries with that shake!" Corliss gave him a face like "*Not* a good time."

"Wait a second," said Max, beginning to do the math in his head as he looked at their faces. Was there something going on between JB and Corliss after all? Could Corliss possibly be going behind his no-dating edict to date JB? Would she really betray his authority that way? Ignore the edict from above? Flout UBC company policy? It was all too much for Max to consider. "I have to lie down in my trailer . . ."

"But Max," said Corliss, stepping in and talking to him in soft, measured tones as if he were a psych outpatient. "We're on a soundstage—there are no trailers here." She took his hand and gestured around the vast space as if to prove her point. "Do you want to go to your *office*?"

Max felt like he was about to cry. He missed his trailer. And the big mirror in it where he checked his hair. And his toilet where his assistants floated fresh rose petals every morning. His trailer was a bastion of serenity to him, and everything in front of him right now was . . . chaos. He thought he'd made such strides since the first episode. He thought he'd pulled himself together and become the captain of everyone's ship. And the live second episode—he thought he brilliantly handled that, taking *The 'Bu* to the next level. But apparently it was all an illusion. He was a fake and now he knew it to the very soles of his Bruno Maglis. And to top it off, Ellen and Portia had frozen him out. When it all seemed to be getting even darker and stranger in his head, his iPhone rang. He looked at the caller ID. It said OLGA.

"Olga!" he said, answering the call quickly. "It's me, Max."

"Yes, Max," came her thick Russian accent. "I know. I call *you*. Listen, I have question."

"Okay, but it's a little crazy here at the moment, Olga, so I only have a minute. What is it?"

"Da, okay. Can Olga can cancel Legend's appointment today with speech therapist?"

"Uh, well, why would you want to do that, Olga?"

"Because this lisp of Legend? No more. I cure."

"What? You've cured Legend's lisp . . . ?" He was astounded. Corliss's eyes opened wide and she moved closer. "How is that possible? He's been to every speech therapist from San Simeon to San Dimas!"

"It's no problem. I try this and that. Something finally work. We at Tar Pits now. Soon we get hot dog and have more fun."

"That sounds so nice, Olga. Max could use a hot dog and some fun himself . . ."

"Max not so good today?"

"No," Max said, "Max not so good . . . Max very bad, in fact."

"Talk to Olga. Problems at *'Bu*?"

Max thought Olga sounded so cute when she said *'Bu* in her Russian accent. In fact, he was beginning to feel as Corliss felt about Olga: as if she were the greatest thing since hot borscht. "Well, Olga," said Max, moving away from Corliss and the actors so that he could speak freely. "Two of our actors are all of a sudden getting married to each other, and it's causing a lot of commotion on the set."

"This Trent and Tanya?"

"Yes, how did you know?"

"I read on 'Bu-hoo."

Max sighed. Was there *no one* who didn't read that infernal blog? "Yes, Trent and Tanya. And two of my *other* actors are in some fight about some Italian text-messaging business. My camerawoman is on the bus to her foot doctor. And, to top it off, Corliss—my top assistant, as you know— seems to be having a clandestine relationship with one of the actors. And relationships among staff members are strictly verboten."

There was a moment of silence on the other end of the line. "I like this Corliss. She good people. The others I don't know. This I do know: nothing you can do about love life of other people. You direct TV. Not love life. You need to step up, bub. Tell them who is boss. Make this clear. One more thing. Get new camerawoman with better feet."

A wave of relief swept over Max. Everything Olga was saying was so simple—but he'd lost track of all of it. He *did* have to step up and remind the cast who was boss. It was as simple as that. "Olga, I don't know what to say. You're a miracle worker. I'm going to have to give you some kind of raise, or gift, or something. What can I do?"

"Nothing. This work I do for love. We see Brontosaurus now. Call you later." With that, she hung up.

Max moved back to the set, dazed and dazzled by Olga the übernanny. Anushka had returned, a derisive look on her face. Rocco stood with his arms crossed, avoiding her. Tanya had come back, too, and she was blissfully plunked back on Trent's blissed-out lap. Corliss and JB were now far away from each other, pretending like they were strangers. "Okay, people. I'm going to put a call in to the cameraperson's union for a replacement so we can return to this scene in an hour."

"But, Max . . ." Anushka wailed.

"No 'But Max,'" Max said in his lowest, most resonant tone. "There've been a few too many distractions from each and everyone one of you and it's going to stop." The authority in his voice seemed to reach them. Slowly, they stopped slouching, scowling, and bouncing. "I'm the one running the show," he continued. "And it's a *show*, not a wedding hall or a group therapy session or a dating service." This last part was for Corliss and JB's benefit. Their faces betrayed nothing, however—except blind obedience. In fact, everyone was now standing at attention, looking to Max for direction.

"Very good," he said. "Now get some lunch and be back in an hour." They all turned on a dime and marched off to the cafeteria. Max couldn't have been more impressed—by *himself*. He was the real article—brilliant, in fact. And it was all because of Olga. "Olga . . ." he said out loud, savoring the Slavic sound. "Olga . . . !"

# Eight

JB was in the hot seat.

"And what is your opinion of *Project Runway*?" said Uncle Ross, leaning toward JB, waving a tiny shellfish fork in his face. "Does it compel you? Do you record it for viewing time and time again? Do you memorize the inanities that come from Heidi Klum's mouth on a weekly basis?"

Uncle Ross had forgotten Corliss's explicit instructions to sit back and stay out of JB's business. His only purpose was to have her back until she got JB into the hot tub. But did Uncle Ross listen? Never. And now he was in the midst of a full-on gay inquisition—and JB was squirming under the scrutiny. His monkfish carpaccio appetizer sat completely untouched before him and Corliss was mortified. She had already moved on to the entrée—Alaskan king crab legs—and she tore into the fishy meat, taking out her nervousness on it.

"Um," said JB, "I've only seen *Project Runway* a few

times. I mean, I guess it's a way to spend an hour, right? All those creative types on some crazy deadline." JB wiped pretend sweat from his forehead. "Relate much?" He raised his hand in the air answering his own question. "Yes, officer, I do!" Neither Corliss nor Uncle Ross laughed. "Tough crowd," said JB, shifting uneasily in his chair.

"Hmmm . . ." said Uncle Ross, squinting at JB as if trying to read his mind. "You've watched those shows only a few times. That's very interesting." He twirled his shellfish fork, and then pointed it at JB like a judge with a gavel. "But Corliss tells me you have an eye for fashion. *Women's* fashion. That, in fact, you were responsible for her rather startling makeover a couple months back. Stripes with plaids!" Uncle Ross howled as if Corliss's former fashion faux pas were a devastating riot.

Corliss shot Uncle Ross a really mean look.

Uncle Ross jabbed his fish fork in the air above his head. "But you rescued her from a life of that, didn't you? You somehow knew enough to turn this drab Midwestern girl into an almost entirely presentable young woman. That's a very interesting talent for a young man to have."

"Um, I guess," said JB, looking more and more stricken by the moment. "We had a fun day in BH doing the shops, hitting the spa. Guilty on count number two!"

"Uncle Ross," Corliss interrupted finally. "Shouldn't we—?"

But Uncle Ross put a finger to his lips and narrowed his eyes. Corliss knew he was going in for the kill. "Is women's fashion something you've long been preoccupied with?"

Corliss, racked with anxiety, cracked a king crab leg in half and crab junk shot across the table at JB. "Looks like I'm in the line of fish fire!" he joked, wiping the gunk from his nose. Once again, neither Corliss nor Uncle Ross laughed. JB squirmed some more. "Boy, flying crab usually cracks everyone up. This *is* a tough crowd."

"Are you avoiding the question?" asked Uncle Ross accusingly.

"No!" shouted JB. "Women's fashion? Me? Oh, well, I guess we go way back." Uncle Ross raised an eyebrow. "I grew up in a house o' ladies—my older sister and my moms. I was the sole dude! I guess I got trained to keep my eye on hems. Paging Michael Kors!" JB laughed way too hard. "Why—why do you ask?" he gulped, looking like a scared little rabbit.

"Well, JB, I'm just interested in getting to know you," Uncle Ross said slyly. "Corliss speaks very highly of you." Corliss shot Uncle Ross a look that said "careful where you're going with this one." "In a *professional* sense," Uncle Ross continued, taking Corliss's silent warning. "But also in a *personal* sense," he then said, completely disregarding Corliss's silent warning. Corliss made a mental note to kill him after dinner. "And of course I'm a big part of Corliss's life. I secured *The 'Bu* internship for her and rescued her from a dreary future in the field of psychology."

"Uncle Ross!" Corliss interjected, totally fed up. "I have *not* in any way, shape, or form given up on my dream to help people in distress. I've just postponed it a little while I work in television." She then used her fingernail to remove some crab that was stuck between her two front teeth.

JB smiled uneasily at Corliss. Corliss smiled uneasily at Uncle Ross. A moment passed with uneasy smiles and the sound of Corliss nervously sucking yet another Alaskan king crab leg. JB finally broke the silence. "Um, request on aisle seven—where's the little boys' room?"

"Just down the hall, right past the Statue of David replica," said Uncle Ross.

"Right" said JB, "I'll make a left at the marble gonads." He moved his seat back and scampered away. Corliss wondered if he'd ever come back. She still hadn't completely recovered from the Emmy afterparty when JB had chosen the company of Jack Osbourne in the next bathroom stall over Corliss in Versace.

"Uncle Ross," she said sternly. "Stop grilling JB about his sexuality! Okay, so he's a little . . . into girl things. But that's why I like him! You're just supposed to be here to keep me on track for the Jacuzzi maneuver. Remember?"

"Ah, yes," Uncle Ross sighed, leaning back from the table and wiping the corner of his mouth with a taupe Jonathan Adler silk napkin. "The Jacuzzi maneuver! Fear not, my child. I have your back. And besides, I've heard everything I need to hear and I have my ruling on JB's sexuality."

Corliss leaned forward in her seat. There was no finer judge of homo-, hetero-, or metrosexuality in Los Angeles County than he. After secrets, judging gayness or the lack thereof was what Uncle Ross lived for. In fact, Corliss couldn't remember a more joyous time in Uncle Ross's house than the day he decreed that Lance Bass was unequivocally homo.

"Well, don't you want to know?" he asked.

Corliss nodded fast, then closed her eyes as if she were going down a water slalom at Knott's Berry Farm. She was white-knuckling it, that's for certain, and Uncle Ross—evil queen that he sometimes was—was going to keep her on pins and needles. "Okay, all right!" she burst out. "Tell me the verdict!"

"Your adorably geeky little coworker is . . . *not* playing on Uncle Ross's team." Corliss slowly opened her eyes. Had she heard right? "Yes, Corliss, you've heard right! Break out the bubbly and dance in the street! JB is as straight as Victoria Beckham's blowout." Uncle Ross kissed her on both cheeks like she'd just won a beauty pageant. "Aren't you relieved? I mean, I must admit he's scrumptious—in a kind of geek chic way—and I certainly wouldn't mind him playing on *my* team—third base would be nice," he said with a naughty inflection. "But young Master Bader belongs to the ladies!" he declared triumphantly.

"Oh my God, Uncle Ross, that's great!" She leaped up from her chair so fast she knocked over the entire gold-plated chafing dish of king crab legs. "Whoops," she said as fishy gunk trickled down her Wet Seal jeans. Uncle Ross's two new Goldendoodle puppies scampered over to lick at the fish pooled around Corliss's pink Mephisto sneakers.

"Isn't that adorable?" Uncle Ross said, looking at the puppies. "They can't help loving what I love." He shooed them away and leaned in to Corliss with a very serious look on his face. "Now that we have this very important info, Corliss, you can't waste any time. You are to get out of those fishy jeans and into that Jacuzzi!"

"But Uncle Ross—" she said, suddenly terrified the moment was upon her. "I don't think I can do it!"

"Steady, now. Listen carefully to me. I'm your second, right? I'm here to keep you on track. There's a bottle of Bolly chilled to perfection in the Sub-Zero. I want you to uncork it, bring it outside to the hot tub—which I've heated to 104-degree perfection—and get workin' on romance."

"But Uncle Ross!" Corliss said, starting to panic just as she knew she would. "Are you sure JB is straight? I mean, really? I mean, on a stack of bibles—or whatever it is you worship—Zac Efron's eyelashes?"

"Corliss," said Uncle Ross, taking her by the wrist. "You're spiraling just as you yourself predicted. JB *is* straight. No gay boy would use the word *gonads*. Now buck up and *don't* disappoint me. You are a Meyers, after all."

Corliss was about to protest again when JB showed up. "Wow," he said. "That bathroom is off the hook! Who knew Clay Aiken appeared on the cover of *People* magazine *seven* times?"

"Yeah," said Corliss, throwing her head back and laughing so fake-hard that she started to really snort. "Who knew?!"

## Uncle Ross's Backyard—7:46 P.M.

Corliss didn't know how she'd managed to pull it off—but there they were. JB and Corliss. Sipping champagne in the hot tub—and naked as, well, two naked teens in a hot tub. Actually, Corliss wasn't totally naked. At the last crucial moment she'd refused to part with her bikini bottom, and she kept one arm clamped tightly around what Uncle Ross called her "almost chest." JB, however, had gone the whole way. But his fist was pressed so hard over his naughty bits that a vein throbbed in his forehead.

"This is fun," said JB in a way that didn't seem like he was having so much fun. More like in a way that sounded to Corliss like he was about to be shot by a firing squad. Then she wondered if firing squads still existed. Because if they did, she might want to hire them to kill *her* because she was naked in a hot tub! Then she spent a few more minutes following the crazy train in her head back to what JB had said so she could respond to it without sounding like there was a crazy train in her head.

"It *is* fun!" shouted Corliss at a deafening level.

"Right?!" shouted JB, matching her ear-crushing volume. "I mean, what kid my age *doesn't* want to end up naked in a hot tub?!" He cackled like a bipolar outpatient and chugged what was left of his champagne. "Tell me again, Ms. Meyers," he said, wiping the bubbly from his chin (since he'd missed his mouth), "how exactly did we get into this here nekkid situation?"

Corliss shrugged and tried desperately to appear like the entire business was perfectly normal—but her face kept contorting into odd grimaces that she couldn't control. The truth was, she *didn't know* exactly how it had happened. The last thing she remembered was Uncle Ross shoving his best bottle of Bolly in her hand and giving her a way-too-hard push toward the hot tub. After that, everything went entirely black.

Had she slipped on one of the Indian slate tiles that surrounded the pool and awakened to find herself the kind of girl who gets naked in a hot tub? If she had, she wanted her old self back. Her skin was starting to pucker from being submerged in 104-degree water and her bikini bottom was beginning to chafe her thigh. Not to mention her reputation, which was now officially blown to bits if JB told anyone about this.

"Beats me!" Corliss finally belted to the heavens, before slamming the dregs of her champagne. As soon as it hit her stomach, she felt a kind of wooziness she hadn't felt since the time she'd raided the fridge at Cracker Barrel and eaten three entire horseradish cheese balls in forty-five minutes. She gave JB a desperate look. He responded with one of sheer panic. Their faces froze like that until Corliss could no longer contain herself. She had to let the truth out. She had to speak her heart! Isn't that what psychology teaches, she thought, as she plunged toward revelation? That the things we keep silently inside only fester and destroy?

"Um, it just occurred to me, Cor—and I could be a complete spaz for asking such a question—but is this supposed to be a date?"

"YES, IT'S A DATE!" she shrieked, flinging her arms wide—and inadvertently revealing her almost chest. JB's eyes locked with hers. Corliss felt her heart pause, as if she had been cryogenically frozen. Their eyes twitched and pulsed in what to Corliss at least felt like an eternity of terrified silence.

"It is?" JB finally eked out, as his eyes slowly headed south toward her almost chest. Corliss responded by throwing herself underwater—where she had a direct view of JB's lap. She closed her eyes against his boy bits as her heart beat like a Timbaland hook. Had she really just revealed her true feelings? Was she actually submerged underwater just inches from JB's gonads? Wasn't the whole tacky situation entirely porno? And most important, how long could she stay underwater before blacking out?

She knew she had to pull herself together. How bad could it be? She'd clarified her intentions. If JB thought less of her because of it, that was *his* problem, not *hers*. Besides, JB wasn't all that and a can of Pringles. He belonged to the same freaks-and-geeks club Corliss did. So why was she flipping out so much?

Corliss resolved to open her eyes, look JB straight in the crotch, and wait for his response. She'd come to the brink of hot-tub nudity—not her proudest moment—but she wasn't going to turn back now. She took one gigantic breath as she emerged from under the jets, rearing back like some unhinged sea monster. What she saw in front of her gave her an immediate answer: JB's clothes—and JB himself—were gone. All that was left of him were wet footprints that led across the Indian slate toward the house. There, Uncle Ross stood on the lanai with a very sad look on his face.

"Gone?" Corliss managed.

Uncle Ross nodded. "He said he remembered something important he had to do. He seemed in quite a state so I lent him the Bentley. Somewhere on the 405 there's a wet, terrified teen heading for the Valley in a $400,000 car . . ."

## The 'Bu Soundstage—11:21 A.M., the Next Morning

"Who are these people?!" Max called to his assistants, who were standing at attention at his side. The assistants shrugged in unison at the droves of unidentified people scampering around the set. These hyperefficient strangers were taking measurements, jotting notes, and whispering among themselves with great urgency. They'd appeared out of nowhere about five minutes before and Max couldn't find Corliss to help him get to the bottom of it.

"And where is Corliss?" Max said, increasingly perplexed. She'd been missing all morning. Her car had been spotted in the lot, but so far she hadn't shown her face. She'd been behaving strangely for some time, but not showing up at all was utterly unlike her, and Max was getting worried. "Find Corliss!" he commanded, waving his hand in the air as if he were Moses parting the Red Sea. His assistants fled in various directions.

Left alone, Max tried to imagine what the swarm of whispering, note-taking beings who'd taken over the soundstage were up to. Were they dispatched from the higher-ups at the network, sent to spy on him and report back? Had they come from accounting to see if he'd gone over budget with the multimillion dollar set? They certainly seemed like they were assessing *something*; they hissed conspiratorially and regarded everything in their wake with judgmental eyes. Their every move made Max lurch into paranoid overdrive. Finally, he summoned his courage and tapped one on the shoulder. "Excuse me. May I ask you what you're doing here exactly?"

"Me?" said one of the swarmers, looking put out as he

used his iPhone to grab a picture of a Tibetan finial. "I'm from Joy Etc.," he said with his pointy chin in the air, as if that should explain it all, before grabbing another photo of one of the set's vast Moroccan rugs.

Max's eye twitched. He couldn't imagine what Joy Etc. was. Some kind of cult? If so, why hadn't his fellow Scientologists alerted him to their existence? They certainly looked like a cult: Each of them wore a light blue Hugo Boss pullover. "I'm sorry," Max said, once again tapping him on the shoulder, "but there's no proselytizing on the set. You'll have to leave."

The busy little man with the pointy chin and the iPhone looked at Max like he had three heads. "I think you have the wrong idea about us. Joy Etc. is the most exclusive wedding design firm in Los Angeles," he huffed. "We've just been hired for the Ventura/ Michaels wedding." Max staggered back. His set had been taken over by two hormonally infused teen stars—just as Anushka had predicted. "And now if you'll excuse me," the man said, "I need to figure out how I can possibly transform this soundstage into a place of *joy*. Orchids, tulle, candles, doves," he said, rattling off his intentions. "*J-O-Y*. And frankly, it's not going to be easy," he continued, sniffing at the set. "It looks like Courtney Love threw up in here." He then snapped a photo of a tufted damask hassock. "All of this is either going to have to be covered, removed, or, frankly, set ablaze. Your set designer should be *shot*."

The little pointy man moved off to confab with his colleagues, as they all shared images off their iPhones and made horrified faces. Max watched in growing dismay as they then began to make wild gestures with their hands, as if wiping out whole portions of the set. "Tulle! Candles! Orchids!" they began to yell, conjuring all these things with their hands. And then the chanting spread across the vast space: "Tulle! Candles! Orchids!" The voices rose in unison, creating a deafening cacophony.

Max covered his ears and inhaled deeply. It was either that or start shouting in his girly voice. He knew he had to put his foot down and reclaim his directorial authority—just like Olga said—but he was bone tired. He'd been up till 4 A.M. the night before slamming Patrón with six Nigerian models at the Tropicana Bar. His head throbbed as the people from Joy Etc. chanted their joy mantra.

"Can someone please find me Tanya?" he said to no one because all of his assistants were off looking for Corliss. "Oh, forget it," he said to himself, realizing the day—like so many others in his short career—was heading south fast. Then there was a tap on *his* shoulder. He turned, half expecting one of the Joy Etc. weirdos to engage him in their demented chant.

"Max!" said Tanya, dressed head to toe in a white silk Oscar de la Renta pantsuit. "I've been right behind you the whole time! Aren't these Joy guys *so, so* talented? Their vision of my wedding is, like, totally off the hook! They want to build a hundred-foot-long portico of yellow orchids that will be, like, a place Trent and me will totally walk under! And then the whole thing will open up into, like, *pow!*—this explosion of tulle that hangs in big droopy things from the ceiling! And, of course, like, a gazillion votive candles will be suspended from that droopiness just, like, plopping down from heaven like ploppy little glowy things. That's so joyful!"

"Tanya," said Max, taking her by her skinny elbow and steering her a few yards away. "These people are taking over the set. We cannot have that. This is a working environment—if you recall—and I'm trying to set up a shot."

"That reminds me, Max," said Tanya with her pouty face. "Trent and I decided to go to Bora-Bora for our honeymoon." She folded her arms as if that were an entirely appropriate response to what he'd just told her.

"Wonderful," said Max, straining to be patient. "I hope you have a lovely time," he continued, his sarcasm slipping out.

"Hey, thanks!" She looked at a clipboard she'd been hiding behind her back. On it was a complicated, hour-by-hour chart of every minute of her time from now until the wedding. "But here's the thing—we wanna stay for a few weeks so that means we won't be around to film episode four." She counted on her fingers. "Five or six, or whatever episode we happen to be on then."

Max's left eye started to quiver, which it had been doing a lot lately. He wondered if he needed his prescription changed. It was either that or all the rage he'd been swallowing since this Trent and Tanya marriage thing first came up.

"Are you winking at me, Max? 'Cause I'm, like, about to be a married lady." She shook a finger at him like he was being a very bad boy.

"No, Tanya," said Max through his teeth. "My eye is on edge. And frankly, so am I. Do I have to remind you—and your fiancé Trent Owen Michaels—that you are contractually obligated to appear in *all* episodes of *The 'Bu?* Not just one or two—but each and every one?"

"Wow," said Tanya, looking like that was news to her. "Are you sure?"

"Uh-huh," said Max as his eye flickered into spasms.

Tanya put her hand on her hip and scrunched up her face. "Well, you know, Max, this honeymoon is *real, real* important to me so can't you just, I don't know, show a rerun or something for episode four?"

The top of Max's head felt like it was going to open up, at which point his brains would spew all over Tanya and all the workers from Joy Etc. He cast his eyes around hopelessly for Corliss, but the girl who always saved the day was still nowhere to be found. He was about to creatively visualize Tanya without a mouth when JB sauntered up.

"Max," he droned in an uncharacteristically mopey tone, "do I have to wear this puffy, short-sleeved V-neck sweater in this scene?" He pulled at an oversized fuschia-colored sweater that hung off his still skinnyish body. "I mean, I know the Jeebster is playing Ollie, supergeek par excellence, but give a guy a break. This sweater makes me look like Lardo Retardo. And did I mention the sink in my dressing room is backed up?" he continued. "And that I was called two hours ago and so far all I've done is sit around playing with my Dumbledore action figure? Sheesh, boredom alert!"

"JB," said Max, mystified by this peculiar outburst from JB, who was usually the very soul of cooperation. "What's wrong? You *never* complain about anything. In fact, you're the easiest cast member I have . . . *You* can't be turning on me?"

"Sorry, Max," said JB with downcast eyes, "I'm not feeling so super today. My head aches and everything sounds louder than usual and my stomach is all gurgly."

Max recognized those symptoms immediately. In fact, he had felt every single one this morning after waking with a Patrón hangover. "JB," he said in astonishment, "is it possible that you—of all people—were out somewhere last night *drinking*?"

JB got an extremely guilty look on his face. But before he could answer Max's question, a piercing scream echoed throughout the soundstage. "MAAAAAAX!" The Joy Etc. gang held their notepads against their ears. Then it happened again: a scream that cut into Max like a machete. "MAAAAAAAX!" came the familiar, husky-voiced cry. Max closed his eyes against the onslaught. Then he heard huffing and puffing heading his way—accompanied by the feverish click of six-inch Guess heels. "Anushka," he said, creaking his twitching eye open when the clicking and huffing stopped inches from him. "What seems to be the problem?"

"The problem," said Anushka, "is that Trent Owen Michaels, my supposed costar—HA!—says you're going to run a rerun for episode four! So he and Twizzler over here can surf and sex it up in the Bora-Bora sun. Is this for real?"

"Totally!" said Tanya. "We were just talking about that!"

Max creatively visualized a bloodstream full of Xanax and then said, "Anushka, trust me, I never consented to—"

"Episode four," Anushka said, cutting him off, "is the episode where I get all those hair extensions and become my usual hot self again! There's *no way* these two former-model types are going to screw with that!"

Tanya frowned. "I'm actually *still* a model, Anushka. Next week I'm on the cover of—"

"Zip it, Twizzler," replied Anushka, "I'm having a talk with my director."

"He's my director, too!" cried Tanya.

"Does anyone have an Alka-Seltzer?" groaned JB.

"We've just demolished that *tacky* fireplace," said one of the Joy Etc. people, rushing up to Max. "Where's the nearest dumpster?"

The top of Max's head officially catapulted open. "Where is Corliss?!" he shrieked in a voice so high only dogs could hear it. "I need Corliss!!!!"

Then Anushka, Tanya, and JB watched in amazement as Max ran from the soundstage, careening through the vast space making unearthly sounds, knocking Joy Etc. workers to the ground as he went.

## Max's Office at the UBC Network—A Few Moments Later

"Corliss?" Max said, approaching a soggy ball of teenager curled up in a fetal position on his eggplant-colored leather sofa. "Is that *you*?"

"Yes," came a sniffling voice that did sound like Corliss's. "What's left of me . . ." She pulled herself up and hugged her knees. Her eyes were puffy, the color of bubble gum. Wads of Kleenex fell from her lap and rolled off the sofa to the rug. She picked up the Kleenex closest to her and blew her nose with it. The sound that emerged sounded like a six-car pileup on the 101 freeway.

Max's gag reflex kicked in. He hated anything to do with sinuses. But he could tell Corliss was obviously in distress. He'd never seen her this way—and he didn't know what to do. People rarely showed real emotion in his presence, and when they did it confused him. Still, he did feel *something* stir in the remote corners of his heart, and he knew he had to somehow comfort her. "Corliss, what's wrong? Why are you recycling Kleenex?"

Corliss wiped her eyes and sat up straight. "Oh, it's nothing, Max," she said evasively. "I just had a kind of sleepless night, that's all." She smiled a reassuring smile through her puffiness—and then burst into big, heaving sobs. "Ugh! I'm so sorry, Max! This is so embarrassing!"

"Um," he said, trying not to retch as Corliss grabbed the balls of Kleenex from the floor and smashed them all over her face in an effort to staunch her blubbering. "Do you want me to call an ambulance?"

"No!" she wailed as she leaped to her feet and ran from the room. "I just want my life as I know it to be over!"

Max thought this was an overly dramatic response to one night of bad sleep. Could it be that something else was bothering Corliss? Something more important than eight solid hours of Zs? And what would he do now that his number-one assistant was in some kind of emotional freefall? As he pondered all this, his phone rang. After a moment or two of trying to remember how to answer it, he finally connected the call.

"Hello," came a familiar Russian-accented voice. "This is Nanny Olga."

"Olga!" Max cried out, immediately comforted by the sound of her voice. "Is everything okay?"

"Everything a-okay, Max," she said in her reassuring voice. "One question. Can I take Saturday off? My sister Varniska is visit from Siberia. Wants to hit Tahoe. Can you spare Olga?"

"Of course, you've gone above and beyond the call of duty, Olga. Take the day off."

"Thanks, Max. I go now. A little tired. Today I teach Legend to ride bike. He very good. Only hit one tree."

"Olga, you are a miracle worker! Legend couldn't even cut his own French toast two weeks ago and now he's riding a bike . . . Everything you put your mind to, you succeed. Can I trouble you to discuss my professional problems again? You were so helpful with advice last time."

"Tell Olga professional problems. I got ten minutes. Legend is taking nap."

"Well, it's this wedding between two of my stars. I consented to having it on the set and it's totally disrupting the filming of our third episode!"

"Answer to problem simple," she replied in her distinctive syntax. "You tell these two young people they have wedding in catering hall. Like normal people. Set is place for TV. Also," she continued, "you should look at hair in mirror. Olga see you look at hair in mirror and when you do it make you strong like bull. Now I go. Need to watching my stories on TV." The line disconnected.

Max looked at his phone as if it were an instrument of enlightenment. It connected him to Olga, perhaps the wisest woman he'd ever met. He did as she told him: He turned to look at his hair in the mirror over his desk. To his astonishment, after all he'd been through that morning—not to mention the shots he'd done with those six Nigerian models the night before—he saw that his hair looked delectably good: chopped and glistening, pointing this way and that, like a spiky desert cactus after a rainfall.

He took a deep breath, restored. Olga had once again saved the day. He was going to march back to the set and tell Trent and Tanya that all the Joy had to go—from the set of *The 'Bu*, anyway. He pulled himself together and reminded himself of the mantra that had carried him through the madness of the first two episodes of filming: *The Awesomeness of* The 'Bu! He chanted this very phrase to himself as he headed back to the set, recharged and ready to take care of business. He knew that anyone in Hollywood with hair such as his had the power to *move mountains*. And he had Olga to thank for reminding him of this.

## The Set—1.37 Seconds Later

"*Out!*" Max said, casting his arms this way and that, banishing Joy Etc. workers as he went, not raising his voice in the least, yet somehow managing to exude an unmistakable authority. His assistants followed behind in a perfect V-formation, casting their arms wide just like Max. They were a Missoni-clad army and they were winning the battle.

"But, Max . . ." Tanya whined as her wedding designers fled like geese after a shotgun blast.

"Yeah, Max . . . ?" said Trent, who was now on set, high up on a ladder, helping one of the Joy Etc. workers hang twenty yards of apricot tulle over the demolished fireplace.

"Tanya and Trent," Max responded as he came closer, swatting Joy Etc. workers away with a wave of his hands, "the time has come for me to offer an edict. Do you know what an edict is?"

"An edict," said Rocco, looking up from a heavily notated copy of *Madame Bovary*, "is when someone in authority—"

"Rocco," snapped Max, "I asked Trent and Tanya. Tanya? Trent? An edict?"

Tanya and Trent's faces reflected a blankness usually seen on Xerox paper. Tanya finally brightened and raised her hand like a schoolgirl. "Is it a penis?"

"No, Tanya," said Max, wondering how on earth Tanya managed to turn off her alarm clock in the morning, let alone have a career that involved walking and talking. "An edict is a *rule*. And my edict is that your wedding cannot take place on this soundstage." Tanya and Trent started to protest, but before they could, Max continued. "This is a place of business, not matrimony. We are here to make a television show—one of the highest-rated on TV at this time. Which also means you must return from your honeymoon in time to shoot the fourth episode. There is absolutely no wiggle room on this."

Max folded his arms. His assistants folded theirs in solidarity. Tanya and Trent both opened their mouths to begin arguing again, but before they could, Max continued. "I don't care if you're flying all the way back from Bora-Bora, Tora-Bora, or Bali-High. You will be back in time, dressed in your barely-there costumes, and ready to work."

Anushka applauded and whistled. Rocco rapped his knuckles repeatedly against his book. JB giggled. "Tanya thought edict meant penis!" Max shot a look at the three of them. They pulled it together.

"Phew," said Trent after a moment, looking relieved. At what, Max wasn't entirely sure.

"What does *phew* mean?" asked Tanya, whipping in the direction of her mouth-breathing fiancé.

Trent shut his mouth. Everyone held their breath. Rocco raised an eyebrow at JB. Anushka bit the inside of her mouth to keep from smiling. Tanya's lower lip quivered. Even Max held his tongue, waiting for Trent to say his piece. Finally, Trent spoke: "Um, well, like, it means, like, *phew*. Because, like, two whole weeks in Bora-Bora? Bora-Boring if you ask me. But you didn't," he said, looking away. "You just, like, booked the flight. Which is totally fine, whatever—but what are were going to do there for *two total weeks*? There's not even supposed to be any good surfing there . . ."

"Trent!" said Tanya, looking stricken. "*I* will be there! *This*," she said, gesturing to her long, lean, constantly photographed body, "will be there! Aren't those two things enough for you?"

"Um . . ." replied Trent thoughtfully, before pausing for a long time. Way too long.

"OHMYGOD!" said Tanya as her eyes bugged out of her gorgeous face with what looked to be a painful realization. "You're totally getting cold feet!"

Trent looked down at his feet as if to check their temperature, and then shook his head. "No, Tans. It's just I've been a little rocked since I saw the baby Jesus in your salad. I think it was some kind of sign. Like when you get a sign, like, *whoa.*"

Tanya's fingers splayed wide as a scarecrow's. Then she blew. "OHMYGOD, TRENT, THAT WAS A *GOOD* BABY JESUS SIGN! IT MEANT THE BABY JESUS WAS, LIKE, ALL '*GO, TRENT AND TANYA!*'"

Max stepped between them. "Tanya, Trent, please take this discussion to your dressing rooms," he said firmly.

"No, Max!" said Tanya with a look of horror on her face. "I will not take this discussion to my dressing room, because there's no more discussion! THE WEDDING IS OFF!"

And so was Tanya, clattering across the soundstage, a blur of white silk and despair.

# Nine

ROCCO was plunked down on one of the built-in Eames leather sofas that outlined the living area of Anushka's trailer. Anushka had asked him to rehearse with her, but for the last couple of minutes all he was doing was staring at the floor, combing through his inky black hair with his thick, dark fingers. He'd been like this for some moments and Anushka was doing her best not to lose her legendary temper.

"What's the prob, Rocs?" growled Anushka, not able to hide her impatience. She was standing in the middle of her trailer in full costume—stretch box-cut BCBG shorts, a pumpkin-colored halter, and Jimmy Choos. She was also in her bald cap—once again somehow managing to look bald yet beautiful. "Look," she finally said, "if you don't want to rehearse, just say so. But you know that Max isn't going to give us any help with the scene—that's why we're *reshooting* the entire thing." She looked toward the sky as if asking for a witness. "Three episodes into this show and that wannabe *still* doesn't know what he's doing . . ."

"It's not that I don't want to rehearse, Anushka," said Rocco vaguely. "It's that I'm somehow challenged by the intricacies of the scene . . ."

"Oh, puh-lease," sighed Anushka, throwing her hands in the air. "We're not exactly performing *Antony and Cleopatra!* Just say the lines, give 'em your signature tortured Italian-stallion look, and make sure your hair looks pretty. Now, come on—stand up." Rocco did as he was told. "Now feed me your first line."

"Um," Rocco stammered uncharacteristically, rotating his big biceps forward and back as if loosening up his body might help jump-start the scene. Anushka gave him a look that said, "Are you going to start or what?" Finally he opened his mouth, speaking in the slow, deep cadences of his dreamy character Ramone. "Even shorn of your beautiful locks, Alecia," Rocco said slowly and deeply, bending over Anushka/Alecia and taking her in his arms, "you still manage to—to—" And then he stopped. Anushka held her breath. When she saw he couldn't figure out the word that came next, she mouthed *captivate.* "Captivate!" he spit out, looking relieved.

Anushka rolled her eyes and then pulled Rocco/Ramone's grip around her tighter. Out of habit, she tossed her bald head back. She still wasn't used to not having hair to toss. "Where I'm going, looks don't matter."

Rocco stared at her blankly—as if there was no one home. She couldn't believe it. He was simply not about to say his next line. "Rocs, what gives? You totally knew these lines the first time we shot the freakin' scene."

"Mea culpa," said Rocco, releasing his grip, which caused Anushka to slide to the floor.

"Excuse me? On the floor here?" she protested, but Rocco just stared into space, his eyes narrowing, his fists clenching. Anushka got to her feet and brushed herself off. "What's with you, dude? This scene is totally simple and you're the smartest person I know. I say, 'Where I'm going looks don't matter' and you say, 'I see someone's in a dramatic mood.' How hard is that? Not very!" She put his arm around her waist again and leaned far back, waiting for him to say the line she'd just fed him.

Rocco erupted. "Can't you see how this is tearing at my soul????" He dropped Anushka to the floor again.

Anushka bared her teeth. "That is *so* not the line." She scrambled to her feet. There was fire in her eyes as she felt a bruise rising on her million-dollar *tuchus*. But the fire in her eyes was nothing compared to the fire in Rocco's eyes. He looked like a man possessed. The thick veins in his massive arms were bulging as if lava were flowing through them. Anushka took a step back.

"I'm not talking about the line, Anushka!" Rocco bellowed. "I'm talking about myself! Rocco DiTullio, scion of a famous filmmaking family, spending my days reciting cheeseball lines on a TV show so tawdry, tasteless, garish, and vulgar that it manages to take popular culture back twenty years! And for what? So I can pay the bills while living as a frustrated auteur? The indignity!"

"Okay, look," Anushka said in a soothing voice as she led him back to the sofa while checking the extent of her butt bruise with a hand mirror. "I only understood about half the words you just said there, but I think I get the gist. You're an *artist*. And you think you're lowering yourself. I have two words for you: *what ever*. You can sort that out with some shrink, Rocs. In the meantime, hit your mark, say your line, and don't drop your costar! Are we reading each other?"

She waited for him to say yes. Or no. Or *something*. But he just stood there, quivering at first and then, after a moment, rattling like a tall building in an earthquake. Anushka put down her hand mirror and stepped back. Something inside her told her to be afraid—be very afraid. It was at that precise moment that Rocco made a sound—a sound that started somewhere in the depths of his massively muscular body and proceeded upward, a sound that sounded a little like a sleeping lion who'd just been stepped on.

"Indigestion?" inquired Anushka, now officially scared out of her wits at the quivering mass of boy muscle clenching his fists just inches from her. She scrambled backward, trying to find the door to her trailer without taking her eyes off Rocco—but he was too fast for her. He leaped over her in a flash, reaching for the door before she did and—in the process of bolting from the trailer—he tore it off its hinges.

## Rocco's Trailer—Ten Minutes Later

Anushka stood in the sand outside Rocco's trailer. The

hot afternoon sun bore into her bare shoulders, but she felt a chill nonetheless. Rocco was obviously in deep doo-doo, that was clear enough, and she was maybe the only one on the set who could help him. That's because she was convinced they were more alike than they'd ever want to admit. She rapped on the door quietly. "Rocs? It's me. I think we need to talk."

"Is it just you?" came an uncharacteristically chastened voice from within.

"Just me, yeah." After a moment, the door opened. Rocco, eyes downcast, gestured for Anushka to enter. She'd never been inside Rocco's trailer before and she was amazed— but not surprised—to see that it had been decorated exactly like the inside of a library, with shelves of books and comfy chairs and reading lamps. So masculine, so smart—just like Rocco. *If only he weren't such a snob*, she thought as she entered, *I could be really turned on by this dude. . . .*

She took a seat on a tufted brown leather Ralph Lauren armchair and crossed her legs, assuming a stern yet maternal pose she'd co-opted from one of her former rehab counselors. She gestured for Rocco to sit across from her. He did. "Look," she said. "I know what this is about." Rocco was about to give her his signature arrogant look that said *you can't possibly know*. "And before you give me that look like you're all alone in your little smarty-pants world, let me just say something."

"What is it?" said Rocco respectfully, looking impressed by her tone.

"It's about you being frustrated you can't get your movie off the ground, right?" Rocco sighed a sigh that said it all. "You want to be a director, but no one is going to give some hunk with big pecs and no directing experience a shot— no matter *what* family he comes from." Rocco gave a sad little nod. Anushka continued, leaning forward. "And so instead of fighting harder to get where you wanna go, you've taken the easy route again, haven't you?"

"What do you mean?" said Rocco, looking afraid at what her answer might be.

"I mean 'roids," Anushka said, looking him directly in the eye. "Don't lie to me, Rocs. You feel totally sucky about yourself and you don't want to. You want to feel all strong and Rocco-y—but even better. So you turn to the 'roids! You're back on the stuff again, aren't ya?"

Rocco turned away, his face darkened. "How—how did you know?"

"Puh-lease. Don't tinkle on my bikini and tell me it's a sun shower. It's Anushka you're talking to here! Your neck's the size of a dumpster and your arms are as big as Rosie O'Donnell's thighs. "

Rocco put his head in his hands. "I'm so ashamed, Anushka . . . I've let myself and everyone down yet again. What shall I do?"

"Here's what you shall do," she said, placing her hand on his knee. "You're gonna call this doctor I know who specializes in addiction. He ain't cheap, but it's your health you're talking about here, right? Maybe even your stupid career, too."

Rocco looked up. "A doctor? Like a psychiatrist? I don't know, Anushka. I've always looked within for my strength . . ."

"Yeah, well maybe it's time you looked *without*. Take it from me. Sometimes we all need a little help." Then she gave him a big wink to show she was in his corner. "And if you ever mention this moment to anyone, Rocco DiTullio, do NOT say I was wearing a bald cap and looking fugly. 'Cause I will freakin' kill you."

"You can count on me, Anushka," he said.

"That makes one DiTullio I can count on," she said ruefully. "Your cousin totally played me! Total tonsil hockey the first night I met him, but then not one text message since! He even declined my Facebook invite, the creep. Ouch. Experiences like that can affect a girl's self-esteem."

Rocco looked embarrassed. "I love Patrizio because he's family, but the truth is he's a bit of a player. You know what, it's his loss. You're smart and funny and totally smokin'— he's lucky you even breathed in his direction."

"Well, thanks for the compliment. Though it's hard to believe anyone could see me with this cap on and still think I'm smokin'."

"*Au contraire*, mademoiselle, the bald hat just accentuates your beauty."

"Ya think so?" Anushka asked, as she absentmindedly patted her head.

"I do. And I'm sorry about my cousin. I guess I should have warned you about him."

"Well, why didn't ya?"

A grin crept across Rocco's face. "I think I was too busy warning him about *you*."

"Ugh, you are the worst!" said Anushka, laughing and pelting Rocco playfully.

"Ow, watch the hair!" he teased.

"Well, whaddya know?" said Anushka, standing back with her hands on her hips. "Rocco and Anushka are actually paying each other compliments and getting along."

"Huh. I guess that's never happened before . . ." he said thoughtfully.

"I guess hell is getting a little cold," she responded. "But I likey. Why couldn't we be friends?"

"I see no reason not to be," he said. "Okay, then—friends."

They even shook on it.

"Okay, now do me one more favor, Rocs."

"Name it."

"Let's not tell anyone about *this* little Lifetime moment, either."

"Deal."

## Malibu Beach—*The 'Bu* Set—2:38 P.M.

JB was on his hundredth push-up. His concave chest bulged and sweat poured from his brow, snaking in little rivulets into his eyes, making his contacts swim around like pinwheels.

He wanted to get to a hundred and fifty push-ups for two reasons. The first was he was supposed to be bare-chested in the next scene and partial nudity always filled him with a red-hot terror. The second was that he'd been feeling *the urge* again. The urge to go online and spend his paycheck investing in stocks. Bad stocks, probably. The kind he'd end up spending the next two years paying for. He thought if he could just keep pumping his twiggy little arms that dastardly urge would evaporate. "One hundred," he huffed, "one hundred one . . ." he puffed.

"JB," said Max, casting a shadow over him as he arrived, "please cease. We don't want you breaking anything, even though we're insured. We're behind again because Rocco—of all people—refuses to come out of his trailer, and I need to shoot your big scene now."

"Almost there, Max! One hundred seven, one hundred eight—uh-oh."

Max knelt in the sand, putting his face against JB's. "You pulled one of your scrawny little muscles, didn't you?", he said. "I knew it . . . Where is the set nurse?" he called to his assistants, who promptly stirred up a sandstorm as they scampered off to find the set nurse.

"Hold the ambulance!" said JB, collapsing to the ground in a puddle of his own sweat. "I didn't pull anything, I just lost a contact . . ."

"Thank God," said Max, walking away immediately, leaving JB half-blind and facedown in the sand. "And if you see Corliss," he said as he went, "please tell her to come to my trailer. She is once again missing in action. I swear, half the time directing is like herding kittens . . ."

"Righto," said JB with a mouthful of sand. He pulled

himself up and brushed himself off. He was going to need a quick shower before he shot his big scene. He started in the direction of his trailer, but he didn't get far with only one functioning eye. That's when he thought he saw her. Corliss. In the parking lot, about a half mile away. At least he thought it was Corliss. The afternoon sun was high in the sky and he struggled to focus on the figure in the lot.

Whoever it was, she was talking to someone. JB squinted hard with his one functioning eye. It *was* Corliss. And she was talking to . . . a guy. He couldn't see who it was, but he didn't like what he saw. In fact he *so* didn't like what he saw that he staggered back, just like the time in junior high he was bodychecked behind the gym by the captain of the girls' lacrosse team. All the air went out of him, and his blood tingled all over.

He'd never felt such a feeling before, but he had a hunch what it was. "Oh my God . . ." he said aloud. "I think I'm . . . jealous!" Which could only mean one thing: that he had a crush on Corliss. "Oh my God . . ." he muttered again as the truth finally hit him. "Oh my God!" he said again, unable to stop repeating himself. Then something occurred to him that was unlike anything that had ever occurred to him in the entirety of his eighteen years. "When I find out who she's talking to, I'm gonna pulverize that dude!"

## The Parking Lot—Continuous

Corliss shook her head and adjusted the lacy white

halter Anushka had lent her. She knew it wasn't an appropriate item to be wearing for the particular conversation she'd been having, but she felt sorta sexy in it. "Petey," she said as gently as she could to the underage writer standing in front of her with a wad of coleslaw caught in his gums, "it's just—the thing is—you and me—me and you—it's not—it will never—"

"What you're saying," Petey droned, his raccoon eyes bloodshot, "is that Max can make all the rules he wants prohibiting dating among the staff, but that even if you and I weren't on staff, it's not happening between you and me, it's never going to be happening between you and me, and I should pack up my pathetic little heart and store it away forever."

"Well, I wouldn't go that far . . . but yes." Corliss felt terrible. She'd been putting off Petey for the last bunch of weeks, but she finally wanted to tell him the news he needed to hear. "Petey, I want you to know that aside from a little personal hygiene problem, and an attitude that would make Dracula seem cheerful in comparison, you're a pretty cool guy. I'm sure you'll meet a nice girl who will appreciate that!"

"But—but—what am *I* supposed to do until then?" said Petey, looking for the first time like the seventeen-year-old he really was. "I go to bed at night thinking of you, I get up in the morning thinking of you, I spend the *all the minutes in between* thinking about you . . ."

"Gee," said Corliss, "that's quite a round-the-clock tribute, Petey. But what I think you're supposed to do is, well, set me free. Just like that bumper sticker says."

"What bumper sticker?" said Petey.

"The one that says 'If you love something, set it free. If it comes back to you it's yours, if it doesn't, it never was.'" She batted her eyes to drive the point home.

Petey pouted. "I hate that bumper sticker. But I'll try it, Corliss, if that's what you want."

"Thanks, Petey." She linked her arm in his and gestured that they should head back to the set. "I happened to come across your file today when I was doing payroll—so I know your eighteenth birthday is just around the corner. You know what that means?" Petey shook his head. Corliss patted his arm maternally. "It means it's time to let go of the stuff that's not working for you and grow up and be a professional."

"Ya think?" Petey didn't look so sure.

"I'm a big believer in you, Petey," she said. "Any high-school dropout who can pass himself off as a Harvard grad *has* to have something going for him." Petey, basking in this praise, broke out in the biggest smile Corliss had ever seen on him.

"Okay, Corliss, thanks for your honesty," he said, gazing at her like she was heaven in a halter, "whatever you say." With that, Corliss gave him a nudge in the direction of the writers' trailer and off he ran, a blur of black. "Phew," she said, relieved that that was over.

But her relief didn't last long.

"Hey, wait up!" It was JB. She had not spoken to him since their disastrous Jacuzzi encounter *three days ago*. She'd been waiting for him to call—or text or e-mail—an apology! But an apology hadn't come.

"Oh, hello, JB," she said in her coolest voice possible.

"Hiya and salutations!" he said, laughing like nothing was wrong. "So, I've been meaning to call you, Cor."

"You have? That's interesting," she said nonchalantly.

"Yeah, but there was a big *Star Wars* convention in San Diego yesterday and since I wasn't called to work I just, you know, zoomed on down."

She couldn't believe he was making excuses. It had been *three days*. Not to mention the fact that the evening of the disastrous Jacuzzi encounter was the *second* time he'd run away from her. He couldn't pick up his phone and make one lousy call? She'd bawled her eyes out and now she simply had to toughen her heart. "JB, I'm in a bit of a rush, here. I've got something very important to do in Max's trailer and, well, these *are* work hours." It killed her to talk to him like this, but she had no choice.

"Oh, right. I understand, Cor. Maybe we should talk later?"

"I don't know if I'll be free to talk later."

"Um, is something wrong? I know things between us were a little wonky the other night at Uncle Ross's. Maybe I should explain."

"No need to explain, JB. You probably had to run off to see your friend Jack Osbourne. Or talk to Rocco about his buttery biscuits."

"Cor—"

"No, I get it," she said, wanting to put an end to the conversation. "We're *all* busy people. It's just the way life is,

right? So if you'll excuse me, JB, I have to get back to work."
With that, she turned and headed for Max's trailer, despondent.
Turning back briefly, she could see JB walking in the other
direction. The sight of his bony little body moving into the
distance filled her with despair. In fact, she thought she felt
something deep in her heart crack—and then split in two.

# Ten

Somewhere Nobody Knows—3:42 P.M.

## The Bu-Hoo

It's too delish! With the T&T wedding off, the dramz is through the roof. First of all, now that Tanzilla is going to *remain* a revirginized virgin, Virgin America is wicked mad! Follow that trail of virgins????? As big sponsors of *The 'Bu*, the airline is losing a mountain of free publicity 'cause of Trent Owen Michaels's cold feet.

So guess what, *'Bu* bunnies? Virgin America is pulling their ads from the show! That's right, Goth Roth and the UBC networks just lost one of their biggest sponsors! And all because Trent thinks he saw the Baby Jesus in a salad.

## DONTCHA LOVE IT????

And if that weren't enough goody-goodness, *The 'Bu* cast is at each other's pretty little throats again. Maybe that's because when you can't kiss who you wanna kiss you get a little cranky . . .

Sound familiar, Master Bader???? Turns out the geek with the taste for ladies' fashion might just have a taste for the ladies himself . . . one lady in particular.

## GUESSES?

Let's just say she wouldn't look out of place having a Super Combo pizza at Chuck E. Cheese!

*OH NO I DI'N'T!*

And there's more where dat come from!
The calamity! The conflict! The catastrophic cataclysm!

Oh, MBK loves it when things go bad . . .
'cause it makes me feel so good!

Call me the devil, call me a demon—just don't call me late for the dirt!

Dia*bu*lically yours,
MBK

### Malibu Beach—Max's Trailer—3:53 P.M.

Corliss was in heaven. Her entire world had done a complete 180-degree turn in the span of ten minutes. Meteors were bursting open in her head—and life would never be the same.

She'd just read The 'Bu-hoo and saw the blind item about JB *liking her*! Could it possibly be true???? She was in a tizzy. She ran up and down the length of Max's trailer trying to calm herself. How could MBK know JB's true feelings? Who was MBK?? More important, who was JB?!? He'd been passing himself off as someone not so interested, but that Chuck E. Cheese reference was plain as the pepperoni on their Super Combo pizza.

Suddenly, the door swung open. Corliss gasped. It was him. JB. The most adorable little geek the San Fernando Valley had ever produced, a bundle of twigs in board shorts.

"JB! What are you doing here? This area is off-limits to everyone but Max, me, Legend, and Olga." Her heart was beating ferociously through Anushka's lacy halter.

"I—I—I—" he stammered. "I have to run lines and my trailer is being fumigated because of termites."

"It is? Why didn't I get that memo?"

"I don't know," he said.

Corliss looked at JB's hands, which were decidedly empty. "But how can you run lines? You don't have your script."

"I don't?"

"Nuh-uh," said Corliss. There was a momentary pause and then something came over them both. In a flash, those empty hands of JB's were suddenly all over Corliss! Before she had time to think, they were making out. Wildly. On Max's soft leather couch. Tumbling all over each other like laundry in the spin cycle.

It was magic, wonderful, messy. In fact, Corliss had her tongue so far down JB's throat she thought she tasted his larynx. Not that she knew what a larynx tasted like—or even cared! She just couldn't stop what years of teenage hormones had bottled up. It was erupting all over—and it seemed like that for JB, too. They wrestled each other this way and that, trying to get a better angle, mashing their faces even farther into each other, pressing their underdeveloped bodies closer and closer together. Basically, trying to swap as much spit as possible.

"Excuse me???" said Max. He was standing in the doorway.

"WHA-OH-WAH!" shouted Corliss, knowing it wasn't even a word.

"WHA-OH-WAH!" echoed JB, flailing about as he took in his director.

"What," said Max, "is going on here? In *my* trailer?"

"Um, see, the thing is—" said Corliss, disentangling herself from JB. "JB lost a, uh, contact, right?" She threw JB a pleading look that said, "work with me here."

"Rrrright!" said JB, all Tony the Tiger. "That's what happened! And I think I lost it on Corliss's neck! I mean, the floor!"

"The floor is what he meant!" said Corliss as she and JB simultaneously got on their hands and knees and pretended to tear through the shag carpet for a contact JB didn't lose.

"Get up," said Max. They stood as commanded. "Now sit down." They sat as commanded. "I had a hunch this was going on with you two—but I refused to believe it. And in my *trailer*, no less!—which you know, Corliss, is sacrosanct. It's bad enough that I have to spend the entire morning listening to Michael Rothstein blow a gasket about this Virgin America thing . . . But then to find my most trusted assistant in my own trailer breaking my edict . . ." Max trailed off. He looked exhausted. As if the worst transgression in the world had taken place.

"I'm so sorry, Max," said Corliss, looking at JB for backup. "What can I say?"

"Nothing at the moment," Max said. "Report to the set in the next half hour and we'll discuss this further. I don't have time now." With that he stepped down from the trailer and left the new couple speechless.

"You know what?" JB finally said.

"What?" said Corliss.

"I'll tell you what, m'lady," JB said, standing with his hands on his hips. "It really ain't none of his flipping business!"

"JB!" said Corliss, shocked. "But it's his trailer and—and—he's our boss . . . and I was the one who had him make that rule in the first place because Petey kept hitting on me. Not that it helped. I still ended up having to tell him that there wasn't a snowball's chance in Malibu he and I would ever get together. He just stood there in the parking lot looking so sad . . ."

JB slapped himself on the forehead. "Wait, wait, wait—that was *Petey Newsome* you were talking to in the lot?"

"Yeah, why . . . ?"

JB rocked back and forth, holding his stomach because he was laughing so hard.

"What is it?"

"I saw you guys out in the parking lot but without my contact I couldn't make out who that dude was!" JB rolled around on the sofa laughing. "But it wasn't some dude—it was

Petey Newsome, the King of Lack of Personal Hygiene!!!"

"Hey, it's not that funny. Petey wouldn't be so bad if he showered, brushed his teeth, and got himself on a good antidepressant."

"I'm sorry, Corliss," JB said, calming down. "It's just a little ironic that because of Petey Newsome, I thought I was losing you. Before I ever had a chance to have you. Which completely KO-ed me in the heart department. And *that's* how I knew I was totally crushed out on you."

Corliss's heart fluttered around in her chest like a bird set free. "Do you really mean that, JB?" JB nodded. "And do you really mean it's none of Max's business? Because that was really, um . . . masculine when you said that."

"It was? Masculine? Me? Wowzer. I guess I'll try and figure out a way to say more things like that."

"I hope so," said Corliss, tingling all over her body. "And now I really need to make out with you again."

"Your wish is my command!"

And with that, the tonsil tasting resumed.


## The Beach—*The 'Bu* Set—Twenty-Eight Minutes Later

Relief was finally kicking in. "Thank God you're here," said Max to Olga, who was just approaching, moving confidently through the technicians prepping the next shot.

"You call, Olga come."

"It's been a terrible day. I very much need your advice."

"You ask, Olga gives."

"I'm here, too, Max!" said Legend, appearing from behind Olga like a little angel.

"My God, Legend!" said Max. "I still can't get over how great it is to hear you say *Max*, not *Maxth* . . ."

"I told you," said Olga. "Olga cure lisp for good."

"Legend," said Max, overjoyed. "How 'bout if you try saying, 'Sally sells seashells by the seashore'?"

"Don't be silly, Max," said Legend, turning around and shaking his pudgy heinie in Max's face.

"We cure lisp," said Olga. "Still working on attitude. What is problems Olga can help with?"

"Well, one of our biggest sponsors—Virgin America—has pulled their ads because Trent and Tanya's wedding now *isn't* taking place. The airline was underwriting the celebration and we were going to do a whole cross-merchandising thing with Trent and Tanya bride and groom action figures, et cetera. But now the UBC has lost a lot of revenue because this marriage isn't happening, and our producer, Michael Rothstein, is apoplectic. What can I do?"

"Simple," said Olga, pausing only a minute to think of a solution. "Give this Virgin America free product placement for episode. Put name on everything. They make up revenue like that. Olga learn these things on Donald Trump show about apprentice."

Max was gobsmacked. "Olga . . . that's *brilliant*. I can get the writers to mention Virgin America in the script—and get the art department to maybe put the airline's logo here and there on the set . . ." He did the math in his head. Those few gestures alone would add up to several hundred thousand dollars worth of free advertising. He immediately placed a call to Michael Rothstein. And as he waited for Michael to pick up, he set his gaze on Olga. "Who *are* you?"

"Just Olga."

"Just Olga?" Max said as if that would never be enough. "Just Olga!" He was carried away. And before he knew what he was doing, he'd scooped up Olga in his arms and was planting grateful kisses all over her face.

"Yuck!" shrieked Legend as he shielded his eyes.

"Yum," said Olga, starting to kiss back.

"Olga, my God," said Max, pulling away. "I'm sorry to be so forward. I don't know what to say . . . You motivate me to *do* things, Olga! No one has ever done that for me before . . . Thanks to you the network will be off my back. Not to mention the fact that I've finally got the cast in line—and a new camerawoman with no podiatry issues!"

"Olga glad. Now Olga want more kiss." This time it was Olga who scooped Max in her arms, dipping him low to the ground, planting a big, wet one on him.

"Yuck!" Legend shrieked again.

"Excuse me . . . ?" came a familiar voice. Max scrambled to his feet to find Corliss and JB staring at him in amazement. Behind them, the technicians had stopped what they were doing to ogle Max and Olga. "Max?" said Corliss teasingly. "What *exactly* is going on? This doesn't look like you're setting up for the next shot . . ."

"I agree, Herr Director," JB piped in, shaking a naughty-

naughty finger at Max. "I was just paged to come to the set for my next scene and, well, it looks like *you're* in the middle of a little scene yourself."

Max shrugged, dopey from the ooey-gooey feelings that were currently cascading all over him. "What can I say? It seems like love is in the air!"

"Is that so?" said Corliss, slyly.

"Yes, it is," said Max. "And because it is, I'm lifting the dating embargo for everyone! If I can make out with Legend's nanny, you two can date each other—just not in my trailer. Understood?"

"Understood," said Corliss and JB, reaching for each other's hands.

## The Catering Tent—Two Minutes Later

"What do you think?" said Anushka, standing in front of Rocco, who was just finishing up his lunch at a table in the corner.

Rocco looked up at her bald head and couldn't help but smile. "What do I think about what?" he said, shyly. They hadn't talked since he'd told her that her bald head looked sexy.

"My head. I shaved it," she said, tipping over to show him. "But for real! You said it looked sexy and I thought, isn't it time for Anushka Peters to have a sexy new look? So whaddya think?"

"Anushka . . ." Rocco ran his big hands over her now truly bald head. Anushka trembled as he did.

"Wow," she said. "That feels really great . . ."

"It does to me, too . . ."

"It does to *both* of us, you mean?" said Anushka, backing up a little . . . but she didn't get far. Rocco took Anushka by the hand and led her quickly behind the coffee service. "Where are we going?" Instead of answering her, he kissed her. Tenderly. Softly. As if he didn't want to break her.

"What's with the soft touch, dude?" barked Anushka. "I want tongue!" And so she got it. Before long they were making Trent and Tanya's makeout antics look *amateur*.

After a moment, Rocco pulled away, caught his breath, then blurted out, "Maybe *this* is why I warned my cousin Patrizio away from you. Because I wanted you to myself . . ."

"Rocs, this is class-A nutso, but I'm so hot for you right now I wish I were wearing asbestos panties." They kissed again. Anushka pulled away this time. "I'm going to cure you once and for all of that steroid addiction. Ya know how?"

"How?" Rocco panted hungrily.

"Like this," she said, smashing her mouth against his.

"OHMYGOD!" yelped a familiar voice. Anushka and Rocco jumped a foot in the air. It was Tanya and Trent, heading toward the coffee service. "YOU GUYS ARE TOTALLY MAKING OUT!" squealed Tanya.

Anushka panicked. "It's not what it looks like, Tans . . ."

"Dang," said Trent, "that was hot!"

Tanya swatted Trent playfully. "You are awful!" She turned to Anushka and Rocco. "But it *is* totally hot! You two make a hot couple! And you know what? So do me and Trent! Okay, maybe we're not ready to get married—but we're certainly ready to have a lot of public displays of foreplay. Right, Trent?"

"Totally," he said, before sending his tongue into her mouth like a deep-sea diver.

"Let's all make out!" said Tanya, with Trent's tongue in her mouth.

And so they did. Two very strange, totally hot couples . . .

# ★ The 'Bu

## SCRIPT INSERT #3

EXT. MALIBU BEACH—ALMOST SUNSET

TESSA, TRAVIS, RAMONE, and ALECIA lie on
BEACH TOWELS, absorbing the LAST RAYS of
a gorgeous sun. Travis and Ramone wear
board shorts emblazoned with VIRGIN AMERICA
logos.

                    TRAVIS
          Nice shorts, dude.

                    RAMONE
          You too.

They smile at each other—and at the two
gorgeous girls at their sides.

                    RAMONE
          Life's not so bad.

                    TRAVIS
          Not if you don't think about it.

                    TESSA
          Why bother?

They all laugh.

                    ALECIA
          We better pack up. The tide's
          coming in.

                    TESSA
          Do we hafta? It's been such a
          perfect day . . .

Alecia reaches for her BEACH BAG. It is
plastered with VIRGIN AMERICA stickers.

                    ALECIA
          It's not over yet. Let's regroup
          at my place. Get showers, head to
          Malibu Seafood.

                    RAMONE
          Sounds great. We live in one of
          the most beautiful places on
          Earth. And we get to enjoy it
          every day. But sometimes I
          wish . . .

                    TRAVIS
          What, dude?

                    RAMONE
          That we could go anywhere we
          wanted . . . whenever we wanted.


                    TESSA
          Yeah, like if there was a giant
          plane at our fingertips that
          could whoosh us up into the
          sky . . .


They all contemplate this idyllic wish for
a moment. And then a RUMBLING is heard. The
two couples look up to the sky. And there, in
answer to their wish, soars a mighty VIRGIN
AMERICAN 747. A giant red and white eagle,
rising, rising into the sunset.

## The Beach—Continuous

Max was jumping up and down in the sand. "Cue the plane, cue the plane!" The head of production cued the 747 Virgin American jet to enter the frame. "Are you getting it?!" Max shouted to the new camerawoman. She gave him the thumbs-up. "This is brilliant—brilliant!"

He watched as the plane lifted toward the sunset. As the plane soared over the beach—just as he'd planned it with the Federal Aviation Association—Max saw on the monitor it was framed beautifully in the shot. Everything, in fact, was flawless: his gorgeous cast, a perfect sun—and a 747 doing as *he* directed. Magnificent television AND off-the-charts product placement. He imagined his contract being rewritten the next morning. Another house in the hills! A boat off Catalina! Weekends in Miami!

And then . . . Corliss and JB, crushed out beyond redemption, appeared in the shot, walking hand in hand on the beach, staring into each other's eyes, oblivious to what was going on around them.

"Noooooooooo!" wailed Max, collapsing to the sand.

Corliss turned. "What happened . . . ?"

Anushka laughed her throaty laugh and slapped her toned, bronze thigh. "Doesn't get any better than that, does it? Now give me some sugar, Rocs." Rocco obliged.

"I want some sugar, too!" said Tanya. Trent obliged.

Olga ran up, pushing her big, blond hair away from her face. "I hear Max scream?"

"Olga," Max said, forgetting immediately that a

fifty-thousand-dollar shot had just been ruined. "It's you!"

"It's Olga, Max. What can I do?"

Max thought a moment. And then he knew. "Just hold my hand?"

"Hold hand?" Olga said brusquely. "I do better than that." She took Max by the waist, dipped him low, and planted a long, sloppy Russian kiss on him as the sun set behind them all.